The Billionaire's Back-Up Wife

Kaylee Monroe

This book is a work of fiction. Names, characters, places and incidents are either products of the author's imagination or used fictitiously. Any resemblance to actual events, locals, or persons living or dead, is entirely coincidental.

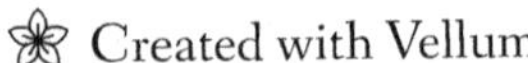

THE BILLIONAIRE'S BACK-UP WIFE

Most eligible billionaire bachelor is looking for a wife . . .

When my father locked down my trust fund until I found a wife, my brother thought it would be funny to add my profile to a new matchmaking app that caused me nothing but headaches and frustration. Romance gave me hives and I had every reason NOT to believe in love, but as a billionaire, and the city's most eligible bachelor that every woman wanted, I'd now become the face of ForeverLuv.

Yes, a frenzy ensued, and I had no time or patience for the insanity.

Deleting my profile proved impossible, so I paid a visit to the woman who owned the business and demanded she remove me. I didn't expect her to stand up to me and flat-out refuse . . . I was a man used to snapping his fingers and people jumping to obey, but this vixen didn't budge—because I was the reason why her waning business was now thriving, and it wasn't *her* fault that my idiot brother pulled the prank.

So that's when I struck a deal with the curvy, sexy matchmaker . . . find me a suitable, compatible wife in one week's time so I could recover my trust fund, and I'd invest in her barely surviving software company. Fail to find me a bride to meet my standards, and she'd have to stand in as my back-up wife.

I swore I'd never fall in love . . . but then again, I'd never met a woman like Felicity Wright. It only took me a string of disastrous dates to figure it out.

FREE BOOK!

Subscribe to my newsletter to receive a **FREE BOOK** not available anywhere else!

Chapter One

Felicity

I was having the best dream.

I was lounging next to a pool with a Mai Tai in my hand, complete with one of those little pink umbrellas and fresh fruit on the rim of the glass. There was movement in the water, and I peered over my sunglasses to see Henry Cavill walking out of the pool. Droplets of water dripped from his muscular form and I ran my eyes over him greedily. The Superman actor smirked at me, and I felt my heart leap as he moved closer...

The shrill sound of my phone ringing ripped me out of my perfect dream. It was a fantasy, really. One that I'd enjoyed before, and I knew that I had just been interrupted before it got to the good part.

Damn it.

Rolling over in bed with a huff, I cracked open my eyes and grabbed the offensive cell phone off my nightstand. Glancing at the screen I saw that it was my friend and business partner, Christine Collins.

I had a moment of confusion. It was barely seven in the morning, and I didn't usually go into the office until nine. Why in the world was she calling me so early?

"Hello?" I croaked, my voice thick from sleep.

"Oh my God, have you seen the big news?" Her voice was way too loud and excited for my *not a morning person* state of being.

"What?" I rolled onto my back again, stifling a yawn. My eyes were still closed to keep out the early morning sunlight streaming in between the gap in my curtains. "I'm still in bed."

"Well, check it out on your phone. Our new app is exploding."

That woke me up. Putting the call on speakerphone, I grabbed my glasses and shoved them on my face. Then, I pulled up the internet and typed in the name of the newest app we'd designed in the search engine. It was a dating app we'd just launched last week called ForeverLuv, and so far the reception had been average at best.

But when the search results appeared on the page, I felt my jaw drop.

"Holy crap," I mumbled, my eyes scanning the screen.

We were trending. There were news articles covering our app, connecting us with Jackson Halsey Goodman III. Everyone knew Mr. Eligible Bachelor, with his fat bank account and the kind of good-looks that made panties drop left and right. He was a big deal in Charlotte and according to what I was reading, he'd just signed up for *our* dating app.

"Do you have any idea what this means?" Christine asked after a moment of silence on my end.

"Having a freaking *billionaire* Adonis as a client? Yeah I have an idea."

Christine was right before. We were *exploding*. With this kind of publicity, we were bound to have tons of people clamoring to sign up for the dating app. It could elevate us to a level of success that we'd been hoping for.

"I'm heading to the office now," she said, and I heard her car start up in the background. "But you're the face of the company. We need you to deal with the media blitz."

I was already getting out of bed. If this was as big as I thought it was, we needed to hit the ground running. "I'll be there in half an hour."

"I'll bring the coffee."

Ending the call, I rushed through my morning routine, excitement and a rush of adrenaline coursing through my veins. This could be our big break, the thing that catapulted our small tech studio into the big leagues. I started The Femme Code two years ago with Christine and another friend, Madison. The three of us went to college together and came up with the crazy idea to start a women-owned-and-run company designing various apps.

It took every dime we had to get it off the ground—which was why I was still living with my parents at the age of twenty-six—and we still ran the business on a shoestring budget, but I honestly loved it. I had my own company. I worked for myself doing something I loved. I didn't have to work a boring regular job or deal with an overbearing boss.

Now, it seemed that we were finally on to something special with this dating app. Why else would a man like Jackson Goodman sign up? He had to see the potential in it.

When I went downstairs, I found my mom in the kitchen, cooking breakfast. It looked and smelled like eggs and bacon. Unlike me, she was an early riser, always up with the sun, and liked to cook for me and my dad every morning. But, I didn't have time for that today, so I rushed through the kitchen and grabbed a piece of toast as it popped out of the toaster.

"Gotta run, Mom," I said, flashing her a smile. "Big day!"

I was out the door and in the garage

before she even got the chance to respond. She just stared at me with wide eyes from her position at the stove. I'd share the news later, once I had everything figured out. My parents were my biggest fans, so I knew they'd be thrilled to hear that the company was finally about to hit some pay-dirt.

By the time I got to the office, Madison and Christine were already there, sitting behind their computers. The office was an open concept creative space. The three of us worked together as a team here, bouncing ideas off each other. We had a mini fridge in one corner of the room filled with bottled water, but that was about it. There wasn't much room in the budget for decking out the space.

Starting across the floor, I'd hadn't even reached my own desk before the phone started ringing.

"That's the fifth phone call, and it's not even eight in the morning," Madison said, shaking her head. "Everyone wants to know if we have some kind of a promotional agreement in place with Jackson Goodman."

"I'll take it," I said, rushing to my desk

and taking a seat. I picked up the hot mocha that Christine had left on my desk in one hand and the phone receiver in the other. "You've reached Felicity Wright at The Femme Code..."

That turned out to be only the first of four phone calls in a row that I took, all from news and media networks, wanting the scoop of how we managed to snag such a VIP client. I assured everyone that we'd done nothing, that The Femme Code had no association with the man or his equity firm, The Goodman Group.

I sensed disappointment from the people I talked to, as if they were hoping for some kind of interesting explanation, something that would sell magazines or serve as click-bait. But all I could do was tell them that Mr. Goodman must be eager to find love. That was the whole point of a dating app, right?

Between fielding phone calls, I had other problems to deal with. It turned out that becoming an overnight sensation came with some unexpected problems. We weren't prepared for this. Hell, we didn't have the budget to be prepared, and our servers crashed after the influx of so many new users of the app. Reports were coming in of glitches and that was the last thing we wanted right now. Things needed to run smoothly for all these new clients.

So, I dove headfirst into trying to fix that while Madison and Christine updated our website and managed all of our social media accounts, which were also being totally overwhelmed. It was complete chaos, and I wished that we had a staff so that I could send someone out to get more coffee. I had smashed through the drink that Christine brought in for me in no time. Caffeine kept me in a good mood on a normal day at the office. Today? It was a necessity to keep my sanity.

I took a moment between phone calls to check our business email account, unsurprised by the full inbox, but before I could get too far into that, the door of the office opened. All three of us paused and looked up. We were the entirety of the company, and we didn't get visitors often, despite having a conference room available for just such a thing.

There was no mistaking who the man was that walked through the doors like he owned the place. I'd seen his picture enough times this morning to be sure that the man responsible for making our app a hit, *the* Jackson Goodman, was here.

I stared at him as he paused in the doorway, his dark brown eyes sweeping over the space. He was even hotter in person than he was in the pictures, and that was saying something. He was tall with a toned body that filled out his tailored suit in a way that made something inside of me clench. I was a sucker for a man with muscles. His skin was tanned and his dark brown hair was thick. He was movie-star handsome, the kind of man that definitely didn't need to use an app to get dates.

So, why did he sign up for ours?

A tense moment passed before Jackson leveled his gaze at the three of us. His mouth pressed into a thin line and he narrowed his eyes.

"Which one of you is Miss Wright?"

Chapter Two

Jackson

I was going to kill my brother.

Chase always had a warped sense of humor but this time, he gone too far. Late last night, he signed me up for a random dating app that clearly didn't have all its bugs worked out yet. Now, I was being associated with some tiny start-up tech company that I knew nothing about. As if I didn't have enough stress in my life at the moment...

Yesterday, Chase and I were invited to dinner at our father's house. This wasn't necessarily an unusual occurrence, though it had been a while since we'd all gotten together. Dedication to work kept the three of us busy, despite being born into wealth and privilege. My father was a trust fund baby, but his dad taught him the importance of working hard anyway, never assuming that the money would always be there, and he'd passed those set of values onto us.

What he didn't instill in me or my brother was a desire to find love or get married. I couldn't blame him after the bitter divorce that he and my mom went through when I was a kid. I was under the impression that he'd learned a lesson from that whole experience. Love wasn't real. It was a fleeting feeling of infatuation that naive people let themselves believe was everlasting.

I knew better than to fall for it, and I thought that my dad did too.

But last night, he'd dropped a bomb.

Out of the blue, he announced he wanted us to get married. Apparently, he was starting to get concerned that we'd never have kids to carry on the family name now that we were both in our thirties and completely unattached.

I had no idea that was even a concern of his. It was ridiculous. I had no interest in getting married. *Ever.* I told him as much. I recognized the smirk he gave me in response. It meant trouble. That's when he revealed just how serious he was. Our trust funds were off-limits until we were married men.

It was a gut-punch that I didn't see coming.

I left the house angry and determined *not* to give the old man what he wanted. But my brother seemed to have a different idea. He called first thing this morning to tell me about the *favor* he did for me. I was the newest member of a dating app that claimed to help people find "the one."

Yeah, right.

I checked the app out while I ate breakfast, cringing when I saw that Chase had added every cheesy romance cliche he could think of about me. My likes were listed as walks on the beach and cuddling in front of a roaring fire. It also said that I was looking for a woman to spoil. *What the hell?*

Yep, Chase was a dead man.

The app got glitchy while I was trying to figure out how to delete the profile, solidifying my determination to sever any connection that was being made in the media between me and the company responsible for the app. The internet was going nuts over this, and this company was profiting off my name, *my* exclusive brand, which I worked so hard to build over the years. That couldn't continue.

I looked up the business, learning that it was a female-owned company located right here in Charlotte. That seemed like a stroke of luck too big to ignore, so instead of having my people contact their people, I got in my Jaguar and drove over to their office for a face-to-face encounter.

I was going to demand that they clean up this mess.

There were three names listed on the business license as the owner, but when I checked out the few press releases available, it was always the same woman mentioned. Felicity Wright.

Well, if she wanted to be the face of the company, she was going to have to face *me*.

Walking into the office building, I checked a list of businesses in the lobby and found that The Femme Code was located on the fifth floor. When I got there, there was no reception area, nowhere to check in and request an audience, but I wasn't in the mood to be polite, anyway. This situation needed to be dealt with *now*.

So, I pulled open the wooden door that simply had the name of the company printed on the front in black letters and walked in. It was a single, open space with wooden floors and white walls, except for the one on the far side of the room with the huge windows. That was exposed brick. The ceiling was high, but that didn't really make it feel bigger. No, this place was small and unimpressive. Three desks were lined up with women sitting behind computer screens and that was about it.

My God, what kind of company did my brother tie my name to?

But I knew the answer to that already. This was one of those start-ups that weren't big enough or successful enough to have actual, real offices of their own. They didn't even have a staff and probably no resources to speak of. And that explained the problems with the app. They surely weren't prepared for the influx of users they'd received when my name became attached to it.

Well, that was their own fault, I reminded myself when I felt a pang of sympathy for them. They should have set up their servers for success from the beginning. I mean, didn't they know how to run a business?

I was about to find out, because I wasn't leaving here without having a conversation with Felicity Wright. Looking at the three women, I found that they were staring at me in complete shock. But there was also recognition in each set of eyes. They knew exactly who I was.

"Which one of you is Miss Wright?" I asked.

The two women on the left turned to look at the one on the far right. She had three computer monitors on her desk, mostly obscuring her from my sight, but as I watched, she popped up out of her seat and I got a good look at her face. Full lips, bright blue eyes surrounded by dark eyelashes, and brown hair in a messy bun at the top of head, seemingly held in place with a ballpoint pen.

"What can I do for you, Mr. Goodman?" There was a slight note of impatience in her voice, like my appearance here was an inconvenience for her.

Well, too bad.

"I need to have a conversation with you," I told her.

"I'm sorry, but I don't really have time for that right now," she said, her tone a bit flustered.

Was she dismissing me? I wasn't sure how to respond for a moment. It was shocking to be talked to like that. I was Jackson Goodman III, and people didn't blow me off. *Ever.*

"*No* isn't an option," I said, not caring how arrogant I sounded.

I smirked as I watched her eyes flash with annoyance behind her oversized, black-rimmed glasses. Then, she came around the desk toward me.

Oh...*wow.*

This woman had curves for miles, and her casual clothing showed them off in a way that made me almost overlook how unprofessional it was to wear jeans and a T-shirt to the office. She was tall enough to look me right in the eye—a ballsy move I found sexy as hell—and as she came closer, I suddenly had the urge to pull that pen out of her hair, watch the dark waves tumble down her back, and kiss her unpainted mouth until she was wild for me.

But that wasn't why I was here. I couldn't lose focus just because Miss Wright had a certain sexual appeal that I wasn't expecting, and it had been a while since I took care of some physical needs.

"*Excuse* me?" she said boldly.

She stopped right in front of me and folded her arms, which pushed her breasts up and together. I would have thought she was trying to distract me if she didn't look so displeased.

"I said that we need to talk," I reiterated. "And if you can't make time, I'll just buy this crappy little company and have my own team of engineers sort out the mess you've made of your dating app, especially getting me *off* of it."

She visibly bristled. "I'll have you know, my 'crappy little company' isn't for sale."

"Everything's for sale if you have enough money."

Her jaw clenched and she sucked in a deep breath, her face turning red. For a moment, I thought she was going to blow up at me, but the phone started to ring, distracting her. One of the other women answered it, and Miss Wright exhaled heavily.

"You know what? Let's go into the conference room," she said, still with that air of impatience that suggested she was doing me a huge favor. "I have only about ten minutes to spare."

"Lead the way," I agreed.

She headed to the only door in the place, and I followed. Once we were seated across from each other at the conference table, I launched right into the reason I was here. I was the type of man that liked to get straight to the point.

"Listen, this whole thing with my profile

being added on ForeverLuv was a big joke. My brother thought it would be funny to sign me up for your dating app since our dad cut off our trust funds until we get married. I have no intention of using the thing. *Ever.*"

"Oh."

She sounded offended, but I was just laying out facts. I had no interest in finding "love". Sure, the app had good bones—I noticed that when I was trying to get myself off the damn thing this morning—but I wasn't going to admit that to her. I didn't want her to try to weasel money out of me as an investor. People were always after my money, and I had to be wary.

"Wait a minute," she said, shaking her head as if to clear it. "I don't understand. Why exactly are you here?"

"It's simple. I want you to wipe my profile off your app and publicly denounce my involvement with ForeverLuv and The Femme Code," I demanded. "I won't have you profiting off my name so that you can try to sell people on the ridiculous notion of love."

Chapter Three

Felicity

I couldn't believe this guy. Who the heck did he think he was, coming in here and making demands of me? And his holier-than-thou attitude irked me. It was as though he believed *I* was somehow responsible for all of this just because it was proving to be beneficial to my company.

"Love is not ridiculous," I said, latching onto that statement to hide the fact that I was internally freaking out about his demand that I cut his ties with The Femme Code.

We were finally getting a taste of real success, and there was no denying that it was because of him. If I did what he wanted, I wasn't sure how much longer The Femme Code would last. We'd been hanging on by a thread for so long, and when I came up with the idea for this dating app, I was thinking of it as our last-ditch effort to make this whole thing work. I didn't want to pack it in and accept failure.

I couldn't let this man get away, or dissolve his involvement with ForeverLuv. No matter what.

"I don't believe in love," he said in a no-nonsense tone of voice. "It's not real, it's just a bunch of emotional crap people buy into. I believe in business dealings, ironclad contracts, and mutual respect."

"Just give the app a chance. You might change your mind," I was grasping at straws. "You said you need a wife? Well, I think I can find you one. Our algorithms and match recommendations work."

He crossed his arms over his broad chest, and scoffed.

"I'm serious," I continued. "I come from a

long line of matchmakers, and I believe in this system. I can find you a wife."

That was *kind of* the truth. My grandma was known for setting people up in successful relationships, and that was actually how my parents had met. They said she was good at reading people, and that helped her see where love connections could form.

"Even if I was willing to entertain this idea," he started, sounding like he was humoring a child, "I'm a busy man. I don't have time to date a bunch of women until I find someone compatible, or to fix your app so that it's worthy of having my name attached."

I was starting to get really irritated with this guy. He was so arrogant and the way he was looking at me—like I was a dreamer with silly ideas about love—was really beginning to piss me off. *But*, the truth was, I needed him on board if we were going to maintain this huge upswing that could finally validate ForeverLuv, and potentially catapult our company to the next level.

It was the first real break for The Femme Code, and I wasn't ready or willing to let this opportunity slip through our fingers.

"It won't take long," I blurted out. "I'll find you a wife in a week."

As soon as the words left my mouth, I knew that I was getting in over my head. I believed in love, and in the dating app, but to find him someone to marry that quickly was going to require a personal touch. I'd have to search the app for a match myself. At least, I knew that I'd have plenty of women to choose from with all the new members who'd just signed up.

"A week? Really? You think you can pull that off?"

I was shocked to see that he was considering the idea. Jumping at the opportunity to keep his profile on the dating app, I nodded. "I'm positive. I'll make it happen."

He arched a dark brow. "Or what?"

"Or I'll marry you myself."

Oh, shit. Okay, now I was just spouting words. It was a ludicrous idea, and I was sure that he was going to laugh in my face.

But he didn't. Leaning back in his chair, he ran his sweeping gaze over me, and I felt every nerve ending in my body tingle to life. There was an electric sizzle in the air, and I felt a chill run down my spine. He couldn't really be considering my crazy proposal, could he?

"Fine, I'll let you try to find me a bride, and if you fail, *you* can fill the role." I opened my mouth, not sure how I was going to talk myself out of this one, but he continued, "But it can't be just anyone. You need to find a woman that will be a good fit. I need to stay married at least long enough for my dad to release the funds, let's say a year to convince him. So, she needs to be someone that I will want to play house with for a while. She needs to be loyal, respectful, smart, and faithful... Oh, and *hot*."

I rolled my eyes. "Anything else?"

"Well, *love* isn't a requirement, if that's what you mean."

I couldn't understand how the man could talk so disdainfully about the concept of love. How could he claim that it didn't exist when so many people all over the world found happiness with another person every day?

It didn't matter, I decided. I wasn't going to waste time trying to change his mind.

I was sure that I could handle finding him

a wife, even with the ridiculously short timeline. There were bound to be many women on the app looking for a husband, willing to marry a rich man that had been at the top of the Most Eligible Bachelor list in the Charlotte Times last year.

"Okay," I said confidently. "I'll find this perfect wife for you, but you'll have to stay on the dating app for me to do it. And forget all about publicly denouncing your connection to The Femme Code. Do we have a deal?"

I waited anxiously for him to agree. With his name attached to this dating app, the future of the company would be secure.

He grinned. "I'm afraid it's not going to be that easy."

Chapter Four

Jackson

She was confident, I'd give her that. There was steel in her eyes that told me she was determined to find me a wife, one way or another. And that offer she made to fill the position herself if she failed?

Interesting...

But it wasn't as simple as all that. To find the right match, she needed to get to know me.

"What's the problem?" she asked impatiently. I was finding that I liked how sassy she was. That defiant mouth of hers was proving to be a turn-on.

"Not a problem, a *condition*. If you're going to do this, you need to live with me for the week until you find me a wife."

"What?" she exclaimed. "Are you out of your mind?"

Damn. I was enjoying getting her riled up a little *too* much.

"Not at all. I'm thinking rationally, which is the problem with you hopeless romantic types. You get too emotional." She glared at me, making me grin. "Think about it. You need to get to know me to choose someone compatible. The best way to do that in a short amount of time is to stay at my place."

I could almost see her mind whirling as she tried to come up with an argument against it. So, I decided to sweeten the deal.

"I'll make it worth your while," I said, tapping my finger on the conference table. "If you pull this off and I'm on my way to the altar in a week, I'll help you out with this little...operation. I'll provide you with a capital investment."

Her eyes went wide behind her glasses. "H-how much?"

I knew that would do the trick. Money always got results.

"Whatever it takes to get you what you need. Upgrade your servers. Hire staff. Whatever. Money will be no problem once I have access to my trust fund again."

I knew that I had reversed positions since I walked in here, but I was intrigued by Felicity enough to give her a shot. Besides, if I had to align myself with a women-owned and operated business it would make me look good. People loved that kind of thing, and as a shrewd businessman, I knew that I needed to maintain a positive image.

Felicity hesitated for a moment, but I wasn't surprised in the least when she nodded in agreement. The offer was too good to refuse. I was usually very picky about what companies I went into business with, favoring things like video games, investments, management tools...things I believed in. I didn't believe in love, but my gut was telling me to take a chance on this woman. What did I really have to lose? If she didn't pull this off—

and I had serious doubts that she would—I'd hold her to her promise to become my wife.

In the end, I'd have my money either way.

"Okay, I'll do it," she finally said. "I'll stay with you for a week."

"Good. I'll have my lawyer draw up the paperwork and send it over today. It'll be a couple of contracts. One detailing that you will find me a wife in a week's time, in exchange for endorsement of your dating app and capital investment in your company. The second one will be an agreement that *you* will marry me if you fail. A year-long marriage, at which point we can divorce or renegotiate the deal. It'll cover financial compensation in the event of a divorce and all that."

"The perfect business deal," she said wryly.

"Exactly. No feelings involved. But I have just one more thing to cover before I go call my lawyer."

She pretended to check a watch on her wrist. "You've gone well over ten minutes, you know."

I chuckled. "And I'm worth every minute.

Now, I'm also going to send over an NDA. It's vital that you keep my motivation for doing this between us. Meaning, no one can know that I'm looking to get married because I want access to my trust fund. My father was clear. No hint of a scandal in the news or else he'll lock down the money for five whole years."

"He's serious about this, huh?" she asked, and shook her head. "Doesn't he know that you can't force real love?"

I couldn't help rolling my eyes. *Real love*?

"He's always serious." I stood, buttoned my suit jacket, and held out my hand. "Should we shake on it? Unless you'd rather seal the deal another way?"

She scowled at my suggestive tone. "A handshake will do just fine, Mr. Goodman."

"Please, call me Jackson. I think we've moved past the formalities."

"Fine, *Jackson*." She stood as well, reaching across the table and taking my hand. "I'll come to your place tomorrow."

I rubbed my thumb across her soft skin. "I can hardly wait."

She pulled her hand away, and I immediately wanted to touch her again, to trace the curve of her hip with my fingers and pull her flush against me. If only the table wasn't between us...

Biting the inside of my cheek, I told myself to get it together. She was going to be living with me, *finding me a wife*, for God's sake. I didn't need to complicate matters by sleeping with her. Although I was positive that she'd be a wildcat in bed. All that fire inside of her had to come out somehow.

Forcing myself to turn away, I pulled my phone out of my pocket and started calling my lawyer before I'd even made it out of the office. I wanted to get this taken care of as soon as possible.

Then, it was back to work, leaving all of this insane love business behind.

Chapter Five

Felicity

"Are you crazy?"

My sister, Rose, was sitting on the bed next to my open suitcase, which I was filling with all the clothing I'd need for the next seven days. I'd just told her about what happened this morning, and the agreement I'd made with Jackson.

"I might be," I admitted. I had been asking myself the same question all day.

"But you're not going to go through with it, are you?" she asked incredulously. "If you can't find him a wife, you're not going to actually *marry* him, right?"

I sighed. "I signed a legally binding contract."

Rose worried on her bottom lip. "This is...I don't know, Felicity. I don't like it. You're going to be staying with this guy for a whole week? He's a stranger."

"I can take care of myself," I insisted, tossing a week's worth of bras and panties into the suitcase.

For some reason, I wasn't bothered about living with Jackson at all. He wasn't a serial killer or anything like that—just an arrogant rich guy that was no doubt used to getting whatever he wanted. I was more concerned with finding a woman that would meet all of his criteria. I had already started searching this afternoon, and there were so many women to choose from that had pinged his profile, showing interest. Hundreds of them, and he'd been on the dating app less than twenty-four hours.

"But...what if you can't find the right woman for him?" Rose persisted. "You've always been a hopeless romantic, a sucker for all that true love stuff."

I side-eyed my sister as I grabbed my favorite pair of yoga pants from the dresser. "Your point?"

"Marrying this stranger will make you miserable."

She had a point. I always imagined marrying a man that I loved with all my heart, one that loved me back, and I had no interest in ever getting divorced. When I got married, I wanted it to be happily ever after—for forever.

"It won't come to that," I said, closing the lid of the suitcase and zipping it shut. "I'll find a woman that's way more compatible for him than I am. I mean, as far as I can tell, the two of us don't see eye to eye on much of anything. He's kind of a jerk."

"A really hot jerk." Rose grinned.

"I didn't notice," I lied, and she shoved my shoulder, laughing.

"You're a terrible liar."

"No, I'm not," I said, and smiled at her. "You just know me too well."

Rose was more than just my older sister.

She was my best friend. We'd always been close, probably because we were just a year apart in age. Growing up, everyone thought that we were twins.

"Well, you tell this guy that he better mind his manners or your big sister will kick his ass."

Now, it was my turn to laugh. Rose probably weighed a hundred and twenty pounds soaking wet and didn't exactly look intimidating with her short pixie haircut and the brightly colored dresses she wore every day.

There was a knock on the bedroom door, and I pulled it open to find my dad standing there.

"Dinner's ready," he said, his eyes trailing over my shoulder to where Rose was sitting on the bed. "Are you staying to eat? Your mom made a pot roast."

"Sure." Rose stood, no longer blocking his view of my packed suitcase, and he frowned.

"Are you going somewhere?" he asked.

My dad was a protective man, which probably had something to do with having three daughters. I knew he wouldn't be happy if he knew about the arrangement I'd made with Jackson, especially the part about living with him for a week. And the possibility of marrying him myself. It was better if I just kept my dad in the dark about the whole thing.

"Uh, yeah," I said, thinking fast. "I'm going to house sit for a friend tomorrow. I'll be gone for a week."

I felt bad lying, but he'd just worry about me if he knew the truth. Besides, Jackson made it clear that discretion was key in this situation. The less people that knew the truth, the better.

The next day was Saturday, so I wasn't going into the office. I left the house late in the morning, driving across town and pulling my car up to the gate of the community where Jackson lived. Just beyond, I could see huge houses with perfectly manicured lawns and tall fences around the back yards. This was the place where the elite lived, the richest people in the city. I felt out of place already, and I wasn't even inside yet.

"Can I help you?"

I turned at the sound of the voice to see that the question came from a man in the guard shack beside me. He was wearing a navy blue uniform and a frown as he looked at my ten-year-old sedan. There was no mistaking the judgement in his eyes.

"Oh, yeah. I just need to get inside."

"This is a gated community, ma'am," he said sternly. "No one is allowed inside unless they live here or are an invited guest."

Ma'am? I was way too young to be a ma'am, for crying out loud.

"I've been invited," I assured him. "By Jackson Goodman."

He pursed his lips, looking doubtful as he picked up a clipboard. "We'll see about that. Name?"

I had to wonder if I was going to be greeted with this man's unpleasant attitude the whole time I was staying here.

"Felicity. Felicity Wright."

The guard took a moment to look for my name, his frown only deepening when he found it. I was guessing that he didn't like being proved wrong. Well, that was what he got for judging a book by its cover. Or a woman by her crappy car as the case may be.

Without another word, he pressed a button and the gate slowly opened. Following the directions to Jackson's house on my GPS, I drove forward, passing bigger and better houses as I went. They all looked brand new, but that could have just been because they were so well-maintained.

I made a right turn, and the spaces between the houses got bigger, allowing for some privacy in-between each one. Finally, I got to the end of a street and found myself looking up at the most impressive house in the community.

Of course, this one would be Jackson's. I'd only had one brief conversation with the man, but I could already tell that he would insist on nothing less than the best.

It was three stories tall with white siding. There were columns on the porch and at least two balconies that I could see. Parking in the driveway, I got out. I could hardly believe that I was going to be living here, even if it was just for a short period of time. This house probably cost more money than I could hope to make in my lifetime.

Gripping the fancy wrought-iron railing, I carried my suitcase up the porch steps and rang the doorbell. It was pulled open almost immediately by a man wearing a black and white butler's uniform.

"You must be Miss Wright," he said amicably. "Welcome."

I stared openly at him as he took my suitcase and stepped back to allow me to enter. It made sense that a man like Jackson had staff, but I'd never seen a butler in real life before. It was so formal, and I couldn't imagine being comfortable with a man catering to my needs. I tore my eyes away from him as he closed the door and looked around. I was standing in a foyer with a marble floor and a grand staircase. It was an open, airy space, but it felt somehow cold in a way that had nothing to do with the temperature.

"I'll let Mr. Goodman know you're here," he said, but Jackson walked into the foyer as he finished speaking.

"No need, Drake. I'm here."

He was dressed casually today, and I

couldn't believe that he was even more attractive in the dark blue jeans and black T-shirt than he was in a suit. It was because the suit hid too much of his body, I decided. Today, I could see his broad chest, the way the fabric of his sleeves stretched tight over his biceps, and the way his strong, muscular thighs filled out his jeans.

"I'll just take Miss Wright's bag to her room then," Drake said, heading for the stairs.

"Would you like a tour of your temporary home?" Jackson asked.

He was more pleasant today, and I felt myself relaxing. "Sure."

If he was going to play nice, so would I. Jackson led me through the first floor of the house, showing me the gourmet kitchen, dining room, and home gym. When we reached the living room, I quickly decided that it was my favorite place in the house so far. There was a flat screen TV mounted on the wall above the marble fireplace and a brown leather couch with matching loveseat. There was a thick white rug on the hardwood floor and a recliner in the corner of the room next to a bookshelf.

I moved closer to see that he had an array of novels on the shelves. Some were classic pieces of literature, like the stories of Sherlock Holmes and To Kill a Mockingbird, and more recent works. I spotted several books written by Stephen King and the entire Harry Potter series.

"Quite a variety you have here," I commented, making a mental note of his reading preferences.

"It keeps things interesting," he replied, his voice coming from behind me, much closer than I expected.

I whirled around to see that only a foot of space separated us. His gaze was on the bookshelf, but when I tried to back up and bumped into the thing, he shifted his eyes to me.

Amusement creased his handsome features. "Jumpy?"

"I just like my personal space," I replied curtly. The truth was that his closeness filled me with a longing that I didn't want to entertain.

"I'll keep that in mind," he said, moving away from me.

I followed him up the stairs, learning that there were two bedrooms and an at-home office on the second floor and three bedrooms on the third floor.

"Why do you need so much space?" I asked as we headed back down to the first floor. "Don't you live here alone?"

"Yeah, until you find me a wife," he said, a hint of sarcasm in his voice. "But I had to buy this house. It's the biggest one in the community."

I rolled my eyes. "Bigger isn't always better you know."

"If we end up married, you'll find out that's not true," he teased, and winked.

"I'm not sleeping with you either way," I said, ignoring the hot desire that flooded me at the suggestion.

"Didn't you read that contract you signed agreeing to be my wife if you can't find someone else?" he asked, canting his head curiously. "There's a clause in there specifying fidelity for both of us. We sleep with each other *only*."

"Or no one," I countered.

He shook his head, but that amusement

remained. "Wow, you're going to make this marriage a nightmare, aren't you?"

"Nope." I grinned confidently at him. "I'm going to find you a better bride."

We walked into the kitchen to find Drake standing at the kitchen island, chopping vegetables. "Lunch will be ready soon," he said, continuing to use the knife, even as his eyes stayed on us. "Would you like to eat in the dining room?"

"I think the patio would be better, since it's such a nice day out," Jackson replied, turning to me. "Are you hungry?"

My stomach rumbled as he asked the question, and I felt my cheeks flush. "Starving."

He inclined his head. "Come on."

Crossing the kitchen, he pulled open the patio doors. The backyard was just as impressive as the inside of the house with an in-ground pool and hot tub. There was an eight-foot white fence around the perimeter of the yard, providing privacy from all angles.

We were standing on a concrete patio with a table and chairs under a pergola and a grilling station complete with a wet bar and a smoker. It was a beautiful day out, with the sun shining brightly and not a single cloud in the sky. Yet, a slight breeze kept it from being too hot. The perfect weather for eating outside.

Jackson pulled out a chair for me at the table, shockingly chivalrous. When he was seated across from me, I figured it was time to get into the reason I was here. After all, the clock was ticking.

"So, why don't you tell me about yourself?" I asked.

"I'm a businessman," he said easily. "Most of my time is devoted to my equity firm and managing my business interests."

"That doesn't really tell me much about *who* you are."

"I'm a philanthropist, too," he added, still keeping his information superficial. "I give money to charities and organize a few events a year to encourage others like me to do the same."

"Others like you?" I repeated. "You mean rich men?"

"And women."

"What kind of charities do you give to?" I

asked, trying to dig a little deeper into this man's psyche.

"Anything that seems important to me. Earlier this year, I gave a half a million to an organization that helps kids all over the country that are homeless or going into the foster system. Last year, I paid for a no-kill animal shelter to be built in Greensboro."

"You help animals and kids, huh?" I didn't bother to hide my smile. "I'm surprised you didn't put that on your dating profile."

He cringed. "I told you, I didn't fill that out. My brother thinks he's a comedian."

"Are you close with him?"

He shrugged. "Sure."

His reply was short, and I sensed that he was putting his guard up.

"What about the rest of your family?" I continued the line of questioning, trying to scratch deeper than the surface. "Any other siblings? Are you close with your parents?"

"No other siblings. It's just me and my brother, Chase," he said, not addressing the question about his parents at all.

There was probably a story there.

Okay, so personal questions weren't

welcome. Before I had the chance to figure out another way to approach this whole getting-to-know-you conversation, which he was making extremely difficult, the patio doors opened again and Drake came outside with our lunch. Making two quick trips back and forth, he also brought out utensils and drinks.

He'd made a chicken stir fry with rice and given us sweet, iced tea with lemon, my favorite drink. We dug into the food, and I stuck to safer topics. Inspired by sharing the delicious meal, I started with favorite foods, learning that he hated seafood but loved steak. Chinese food and pizza were at the top of his list too. Then, we covered his favorite movies, action and horror. I'd already seen his eclectic range of books, so I didn't need to ask about that.

I wasn't exactly getting a look at his deeper side, but it was a start. Hopefully, it would be enough to help me pick a woman for him to meet. Maybe I'd get lucky on my first try and this would all be over in a day or two.

A girl could dream.

In between my questions we ate quietly, but I kept catching him staring at me. He didn't look away when he was caught either. No, he was bold and shameless as he ran his eyes over my face, lingering on my lips.

My body responded to him, despite myself. Heat and attraction flooded my system, and I had to fight the urge to squirm in my seat. This wasn't the way that this was supposed to go. I wasn't here to sleep with this man, no matter how appealing the notion might be. Besides, I barely knew him, and I wasn't the casual sex type.

Finally, after the third time it happened, I felt my frustration boil over. "What are you looking at?"

He shrugged, taking his time sipping his tea before he answered.

"I like to give my dinner companions my full attention," he replied, but I knew he was lying. The heat in his gaze made it obvious that the attraction here was mutual. "You know, you should consider wearing your hair down sometime."

My hand went to my head, smoothing back my ponytail.

"I'm going to spin class with my sister this afternoon," I said, clinging to my professionalism. There was too much at stake here to get lost in the feelings this man was producing inside of me. "So, let's finish our business."

"Fair enough," he agreed, and I went back to learning his likes and dislikes while we finished our meal.

Chapter Six

Jackson

I had a problem, and her name was Felicity Wright.

What was I thinking when I demanded that she live with me for a week? It had only been a few hours so far, and I was already burning for her.

It was crazy, because she wasn't my type at all. I didn't have the time or interest in dating, but every man had needs. Over the years, I'd found that no-strings-attached sex was the best way to find the satisfaction my body craved without the drama of dealing with a woman that wanted an emotional attachment.

The women I took to bed always knew the score. I was upfront about my expectations. And I usually went for women that tried to impress me. They went all out with hair and makeup, manicured nails, and never a hair out of place. Spray tans and high heels.

There was something more genuine about Felicity. So far, I hadn't seen her wear makeup and she dressed for comfort instead of trying to show off her curvy body, but she had an undeniable appeal. It was something that couldn't be bought at a store, and it didn't come out of a bottle. It was all natural.

It was also driving me crazy.

I told myself that I just needed to get laid. Hopefully, Felicity would find a woman for me soon and I'd get the chance to scratch that itch.

After she left for her spin class, I decided that a little exercise could do me some good too. Maybe it would give me a chance to work off some of the sexual frustration brewing beneath the surface. So, I changed my clothes and headed to my home gym.

The room was packed with equipment, a bench press, treadmill, an ab sculpting machine, and a punching bag hanging from the ceiling in the center of the space. I headed toward the punching bag, not bothering to warm up before I started driving my fist into the vinyl exterior, my movements light and fast as I kept my feet moving, as if I was facing a real opponent and trying to avoid being hit. I had taken a kickboxing class years ago, and what I learned there stuck with me.

The only sounds in the room were the dull thuds from the impact and the slight rattle of the chains that attached the punching bag to the floor and ceiling. My breathing quickly turned heavy as I tried to channel all my desire into my workout. I needed some kind of release, or I was bound to pounce on Felicity the next time she was near.

Not a smart business move.

Sweat coated my body, and I paused long enough to whip my shirt off, wadding it up and swiping it across my forehead to keep the perspiration from getting into my eyes. It felt good to pour my energy into this, and I kept it up until my hands ached and the muscles in my leg muscles started to feel tight and overworked.

Still, I couldn't get the curvy matchmaker out of my mind. Frustrated, I went back upstairs to my master suit. I needed a shower, so I peeled my clothes off and stepped into the stall, welcoming the initial shock of cold water from the showerhead before it turned first warm, then hot. The heat of the water helped to ease the tension in my body.

Soaping up a loofa, I ran it over my chest and down my stomach. My mind lingered on Felicity, and I felt my cock growing as I washed it, the stimulation caused by the simple touch combining with the lust that she ignited in me. I knew what I needed to do.

Dropping the loofa, I braced myself with one hand on the wall of the shower and used the other to grip my cock tight. The hot water ran down my back, and I closed my eyes, picturing Felicity. Her big blue eyes, her full lips, the swell of her breasts...

I bit my bottom lip and stroked my erection harder. Up and down, up and down, wishing that it was her soft hand on me. Or her pretty little mouth sucking all the way down to the base of my shaft.

God, I wanted her to be on her knees in front of me. I could fist her damp hair in my hand and guide her until my cock hit the back of her throat. I could picture it so clearly, and it made the pleasure of this act so much better, so much hotter. My breath hitched, and I moved my hand faster. My blood was pounding in my ears.

Suddenly, my orgasm slammed into me, a heated blast that made me release an incoherent sound of raw pleasure. My release spilled onto the shower wall, wasted when it could have been inside of the woman in my mind.

The image of Felicity was slow to fade from my thoughts, and I relaxed against the tile, trying to catch my breath. It was enough to take the edge off, but it wouldn't last. No, I needed the real thing, a willing woman to let me sink myself up to the hilt. Until I found one, I had a feeling that Felicity would be featuring a leading role in my fantasies.

* * *

That evening, I ate dinner alone. I didn't know what Felicity was up to after her spin class, but I didn't want to call or text her to ask. That would make it feel too much like we were a couple.

So, I shut myself in my office, eating a tray of food that Drake brought me while doing some work on what should have been my day off. This wasn't unusual for me. I wasn't great at relaxing, especially when I was in the middle of a business deal.

I was looking into investing in a small motorcycle dealership here in Charlotte. I rarely went for businesses that were so new, since this one just opened a year ago, but the potential for growth was greater than expected, and they wanted to expand to a larger location. I could provide the funds for the move and becoming a silent partner in the business, but it was a riskier investment than I was used to making. This business wasn't well-established yet. So, I was taking my time, doing research, and hoping that I didn't get in over my head.

A few days ago, I might not have hesitated so much to pull the trigger. I was a man that went with my gut and right now, it was telling me to go for it. But things were different now. Without access to my trust fund, I was more dependent on my income from my company. The Goodman Group earned me plenty of money to maintain my lifestyle, as long as I didn't make any bad decisions.

I finished my dinner while I reviewed the quarterly financial reports provided by the general manager of the dealership and pushed the tray of empty plates to the corner of my desk. Suddenly, my attention was pulled away from the information by a knock on the closed office door.

"Come in," I called out with my eyes still on the computer screen, already knowing it had to be Felicity. Drake's knock was different, always three sharp taps.

When she opened the door, I could tell that she was excited about something, and that intrigued me enough to turn away from the computer completely.

"Welcome back," I said, purposefully not

asking how she spent her evening, but leaving the door open for her to volunteer the information. I wasn't even sure why I cared so much.

"Hey, I hope I'm interrupting anything," she said, walking further into the room and eying the empty tray on the desk.

"I'm just doing some work."

"On a Saturday?"

"Whenever the mood strikes," I said, and shrugged. "My business dealings are a big part of who I am, and I can't just ignore important work because it's the weekend."

"Don't you know how to relax and have fun?"

"Have you eaten?" I changed the subject, not wanting to speculate about my own inability to enjoy the simple things in life. I'd decided long ago that this was just who I was and trying to change myself would never work.

"Yes," she said, letting the subject drop easily.

I noticed that she never really pushed me on anything. If I didn't want to give her an answer to a question, she accepted it and moved on. I wished that everyone in my life was like that.

"Rose and I stopped at this health food place for dinner after class. She's trying desperately to shed five pounds."

"And Rose is your sister?" I remembered her saying that was who she was going with to her spin class.

"Yes, my older sister. After dinner, she had a date, but I hung around, using the restaurant's free Wi-Fi to check out the dating app."

I saw that there was a laptop bag hanging from her shoulder that I didn't notice before. "And you were giving *me* a hard time about working on a Saturday?"

"The point is," she continued as if I hadn't spoken, taking a seat in one of the two chairs directly in front of me. She started to pull out her computer from her bag, now a bit more excited. "I think I found you a match."

"Really? Already?" It didn't seem possible, but when Felicity sat her laptop on my desk and turned it to face me, I found myself looking at the dating profile of a drop-dead gorgeous blonde with a megawatt smile.

"Her name is Alicia Bryant. She's a model."

Okay, so she checked the box next to *hot*.

"A model?" I repeated. That definitely made her my type, and the kind of woman I'd dated in the past. "But why would a model be on a dating app? I mean, it's odd, right? A woman like her can get whoever she wants."

She did a cute little eye roll. "Need I remind you that *you're* on the app."

I sighed. "I explained that already. It was *Chase* who added me." Not that it mattered any longer.

"Still, Alicia is beautiful, but there's more to a person than looks. And some of the people on the app are looking for a deeper connection, so that they can find real love and their soulmate."

I couldn't help chuckling. *Soulmate*? How did she even utter those words with such a serious look on her face?

I leaned back in my leather chair and waved a hand in the air. "Okay, fine, tell me more about this woman."

"She takes pride in being loyal and loves

horror movies. Oh, and she is *very* eager to get married."

Well, how could I say no to that? In fact, why was I even hesitating?

I thought about what I did in the shower earlier and nodded at Felicity. A woman, any woman that wasn't her, would do just fine.

"Okay, great," I agreed. "When can I meet her?"

She beamed at me. "I already pulled some strings and got you a reservation at a restaurant for dinner tomorrow night."

So, it was already decided. I was going on my first date in years tomorrow night. I might just be going to meet my future wife.

Chapter Seven

Felicity

The guest bedroom that Jackson had given me was so luxurious that I couldn't help waking up with a small smile on my face. The mattress on the huge bed was the most comfortable one I'd ever slept on in my life.

It was Sunday, so I'd planned to sleep in a little, but it was still early. I wasn't sure why I woke up before my alarm, but I knew that I wouldn't be able to go back to sleep with the morning sun shining in through the skylight.

Yep, my room was on the third floor and had a freaking skylight, as well as an en suite bathroom that was bigger than my entire bedroom at my parents' place. A girl could get used to this level of luxury.

But I wouldn't, because tonight was Jackson's date with Alicia, and I had a good feeling about it. If they clicked, I was sure that I'd be back home as soon as tomorrow and the investment money he promised was as good as mine. Or, well, the company's.

Getting dressed in my most comfortable jeans and a blue V-neck blouse, I went downstairs. It was quiet in the house, with not a single stair creaking as I made my way down two flights in my socks.

My stomach was rumbling since I had a small salad for dinner at that health food restaurant that Rose had dragged me to last night, so I headed to the kitchen. The smell of coffee greeted me first, then Drake did.

"Good morning, Miss Wright." He was wiping down the counter with a rag, and I figured that I had missed breakfast and he was cleaning up. "I took the liberty of saving you a plate of pancakes."

I smiled. "Be careful, Drake. I might get spoiled if you keep doing stuff like that."

"That's my goal." He pulled a plate of pancakes out for me, placing them on the kitchen island with butter and warm syrup. "Coffee?"

"Please."

He poured a mug, placing it in front of me with a bowl of sugar and some cream. Taking a seat on a stool at the island, I started to make the coffee the way I liked it. I looked around the kitchen as I sipped the steaming liquid. I had been overwhelmed by everything I saw yesterday, so I didn't pay much attention to this room. It was a bright, open space with white cabinets and walls. Even the plate and coffee mug were white. The countertops were a grey stone and the appliances were black.

I dug into the food, watching as Drake finished cleaning up the kitchen. It was spotless by the time he was done.

"Where's Jackson?" I asked as Drake took away my empty plate, wondering if he went into the office, despite it being Sunday. The man was clearly a workaholic.

"Mr. Goodman went out to the pool after breakfast," Drake said, quickly cleaning and drying my single plate and putting it in the cabinet with the others.

I slipped off the stool and moved to the patio doors as Drake left the room, presumably to go work on something somewhere else in the house. It was a big place, and I was sure there was plenty to keep him busy.

I glanced outside. It was another beautiful day, and as I looked at the pool, I could see the sun shining off the water. As I watched, the surface of the water broke and Jackson emerged from beneath. As he started to climb the steps out of the pool, he combed his wet hair away from his face using his fingers. My eyes went to his flexing bicep, and I felt my mouth go dry.

I stood frozen, watching him as more and more of his bare flesh became visible. Smooth, tanned skin over taut muscles. My pulse raced as my gaze absorbed every inch of him. The water ran in rivulets down his solid chest and chiseled abs, and I felt an ache in my core as I thought about having all that masculine strength pushing me down onto a flat surface and . . .

I sucked in a breath and tried to shake those erotic thoughts from my brain. It had been so long since I'd felt this hot for a man. I couldn't even remember the last time I had sex. The last couple of years, I had been so busy getting The Femme Code up and running that I hadn't made time for much else. It took a lot of time and energy to start a business, and that didn't leave space for much else.

Jackson was fully out of the pool now, his swim trunks slung low on his hips. I could see the V-lines on his lower abdomen, disappearing beneath the waistband of his trunks and drawing my eye to bulge in his pants.

I swallowed hard. God, he was pure walking temptation.

Jackson grabbed a towel off one of the lounge chairs by the pool and started to dry off. Suddenly, as if he could feel my eyes on him, he paused and turned his head to look my way with a wolfish grin.

Startled and embarrassed at being caught blatantly staring at him, I stumbled backwards, trying to get out of his sight. But my movements were clumsy, and my feet got tangled around each other. My arms pinwheeled, but there was no regaining my balance as I fell backward.

I landed hard on the floor, with no grace whatsoever. My elbow took the brunt of it, and I gasped as I rolled onto my back. I sat up but didn't get a chance to recover any of my dignity by getting up before the patio door was thrown open and Jackson came rushing in. Concern was etched across his face as he knelt down beside me.

"Are you okay?" he asked.

My heart stuttered as our eyes met, and I got lost in his brown orbs for a moment. My lips parted, and there was an undeniable pull in the center of my chest, like a magnet that was attracted to him.

I blinked and looked away, reminding myself that this man was a pain in my ass. What was I thinking, staring at his bare chest and getting swept away by a soft look of concern in his eyes? This was the same guy that had sauntered into my office making demands and belittling my work just two days ago.

"Did you hurt yourself?" he asked when I didn't respond right away.

"Just my pride," I muttered, even though my elbow was throbbing and my ankle had gotten twisted up beneath me when I fell.

Jackson chuckled and held out his hand, and I took it, allowing him to pull me to my feet. But the second I tried to put weight on the ankle that had gotten twisted, pain shot up my leg, and I let out a small cry of agony while clinging to him.

"What is it?" he asked.

"My ankle." I wince when I attempted to gingerly stand on my foot again. "I hurt it when I fell."

Without another word, Jackson scooped me up into his arms and started carrying me through the house.

"What are you doing?" I spluttered in shock, even as I wrapped my arms around him and held on.

"Taking you to the couch. You shouldn't walk, even if you sprained your ankle."

His skin was still damp from the pool and

droplets of water dripped onto my arm at the back of his neck. He radiated body heat and our faces were so close, just inches apart. My desire for him flared again, so it was something of a relief when we reached the living room and he deposited me gently onto the chaise part of the couch.

I was reclined on my back, and he moved to the end of the sofa, pushing up my jeans and pulling down my sock. Just the slight jostling from his movements caused another jolt of pain, but I bit my lip and stayed quiet.

"It already looks swollen," he commented, gently touching the area.

I couldn't hold back my gasp as he probed a particularly tender spot.

He stopped and frowned. "Try to move your toes."

I did, and even managed limited flexing of my foot.

"Okay, I don't think it's broken, but you need to stay off of it at least for the rest of the day." He glanced up at me. "Do you want me to call a doctor? I can have one come to the house."

"Doctor's still make house calls?"

"Well, for an exorbitant fee they do." He shrugged.

It must be nice to have that kind of money to throw around.

"No, I don't need a doctor," I decided. "I'll just keep off of it for the day."

I didn't want to make a bigger deal out of this than it was. Besides, I had bigger things to worry about. Like my raging libido and the fact that Jackson was practically naked, except where it really counted. Even then, the wet, clinging fabric of his swim trunks gave me a fairly good idea of what lay beneath.

He grabbed a couple of throw pillows off the couch and carefully lifted my leg into the air, putting them in place to allow my ankle to stay elevated. "I'll be right back."

I forced myself not to watch as he walked away, knowing that the view of his backside wasn't going to help me get myself under control. *You're here to help him get hitched,* I reminded myself.

He returned a couple of minutes later with an ice pack wrapped in a thin dishtowel.

I winced when he applied it to my ankle, but his touch was gentle.

"No leaving this couch," he commanded, frowning at me. "If you need anything, you ask me or Drake to get it for you."

"Are you going to be this bossy when we're married?" I asked, regretting the snarky remark immediately. I wished I could take those words back, but that wasn't possible. My eyes went wide, and I stammered, "Uh...I mean, *if* we...not that we're going to end up married. I'll find someone else...but you know, if I don't—"

Jackson's laughter cut off my senseless rambling, and the warm sound washed over me, going straight between my legs. I had never heard a real, genuine laugh from him before, and the effect on my body was just like every other part of him. I really needed to get myself under control.

"Don't worry," he said when his amusement passed. "I'll just pretend I didn't hear you say that."

"I appreciate it." I murmured, some of my mortification melting away.

I didn't want him thinking that I was

hoping to be the future Mrs. Goodman myself. All I was interested in was the business part of this arrangement, which I supposed was something that the two of us had in common.

Chapter Eight

Jackson

That evening, I got ready for my big date, feeling an eager anticipation that I didn't usually experience before going out with a woman. Not that I did it often.

Usually, if I took a woman out to dinner, it was just a step in the process of seducing her. I wasn't trying to get to know her. It wasn't a step toward a more meaningful relationship. If I took a woman out, the idea was to impress her, to entice her to come back to my place for the night. I turned on the charm and laid it on as thick as necessary to get what I wanted.

Tonight was different. I was going to meet a woman that might be my bride. It wasn't real, of course. I wasn't looking for love, but I did need compatibility. I was going to be living with the woman I married for at least a year. She couldn't be someone that would drive me nuts or not fit in with my life. I was a busy man, attending charity and work events on a monthly basis. My wife would need to be at my side.

That was one of the reasons that I was eager to meet Alicia. As a model, she wouldn't just look good on my arm, but she'd probably have experience attending galas and would surely be comfortable in front of a camera. The press loved to snap my picture.

I walked downstairs to find that Felicity was right where I left her on the couch. She'd been there since her tumble this morning, and I insisted that she stay in place, despite her protests. Apparently, the swelling had gone down and the pain lessened to the point that she felt like she could walk on it without causing any damage. It turned out that she was a terrible patient that didn't take orders well.

It wasn't until I threatened to cancel my date and stay home to keep an eye on her that she finally agreed not to move around without help until tomorrow. I wanted to be sure that she was okay. My heart had lurched when I saw her fall to the ground through the patio door, and it seemed to awaken a protective instinct that I never knew I had.

Buttoning up the jacket of my grey suit, I walked around the couch and came to a stop in front of it. She was sitting up, reading a book from my shelf, The Catcher in the Rye. Her foot was still elevated, but she didn't need ice anymore.

"Well, what do you think?" I asked, turning from one side to the other.

There was heat in Felicity's eyes, and I had my answer before she even opened her mouth. "You look great."

"Where did you make this reservation, anyway?"

"At a restaurant downtown, The Blue Ember."

My eyebrows popped up in surprise. That place was hard to get into, booking up weeks in advance. It was a five-star restaurant with an expensive menu, the kind of place that only someone with a lot of money could afford.

"How'd you pull that off?" I asked, impressed.

"I have my ways," she said mysteriously. But when I gave her a look, she grinned. "Okay, fine. I know the owner, so I called in a favor."

"You *know* him? How?"

I naturally assumed that he was an ex-boyfriend, and it unsettled me for some strange reason. Jealousy was such a foreign feeling for me that I almost didn't recognize what that twinge was inside of me. It felt like anger, but less defined, and more possessive. I didn't like it and it certainly wasn't an appropriate reaction to Felicity, so I tried to push it away.

"I used to work for him," she explained. "I was a waitress at The Blue Ember during college. Almost every weekend for four years.

I think I probably served every rich person in the city during that time. Probably even you."

I was sure that I would remember her if that was the case, but I didn't say that.

"Well, it's a good thing I went with a suit then."

"You'll fit right in," she agreed with a nod.

Felicity reached over the coffee table, grabbing her drink. The book she was reaching slipped from her other hand, landing on the floor. I came forward and picked it up, handing it over. When our fingers brushed, I felt fire dance over my skin, and we both paused, sharing a moment of attraction and desire.

I knew that she felt it too, I could see it in her eyes. The more time I spent with Felicity, the better I was getting at reading her expressions, which was how I knew that she was going to pull away before she did it. She dropped her eyes to the book as she broke contact with me, and I hesitated for just a second, thinking about how tempting it would be to stay and explore what we kept dancing around.

But in the end, I knew that it was better if I left.

"I'd better go," I said, stepping away.

"Have fun," she said, giving me a small smile that didn't quite meet her eyes. "I won't wait up."

I took my Corvette to the restaurant, handing over my keys to the valet. The Blue Ember was a tall building with large windows, providing diners with a view of the street below. Inside, there were dark blue walls with silver accents. Chandeliers hung from the ceiling, casting a golden glow over the tables.

I was the first to arrive, and the host showed me to one of the tables pressed against the window. I pulled out my phone, putting it on vibrate. Then, I scanned the menu while I waited for my date to arrive. I had been here a couple of times in the past, but it had been years.

The waitress came to the table, and I ordered an old fashioned. Just as the waitress was walking away to get my drink, I saw the host approaching again. There was no mistaking my date at his side. She looked just like her picture. Long blonde hair, ivory skin, rail thin. She was wearing a sparkly red dress with a slit up the side all the way to her hip. Her black heels were so high that I couldn't imagine how she was able to walk in them, but I'd dated enough models to know that they could handle just about any wardrobe without breaking a sweat. Whatever it took to look a certain way.

I stood as she reached the table, starting to come around to pull her chair out for her, but she beat me to it, sitting down and flashing me a smile. "Hi, I'm Alicia."

"Jackson," I introduced myself, my most charming smile effortlessly slipping into place.

She held out her hand with the palm facing down, obviously wanting me to kiss the back of her hand, at the same time that I held out my hand to shake hers. It was awkward for a moment and the two of us chuckled.

"Your waitress will be right with you," the host said, nodding at both of us before walking away.

Alicia watched him until he was out of hearing range before turning back to me and rolling her eyes. "God, sorry about that. Men always stare at me. I hope it doesn't make you uncomfortable."

I furrowed my brow. "What are you talking about?"

"The host. Didn't you notice?" She flipped her hair over her shoulder and gave me an unconvincing put-upon look. "He was *so* obvious."

"Uh...no, I didn't notice."

I was pretty sure that it was all in her head, since the man didn't leer at her at all that I saw, but I wasn't going to argue the point with her.

"Oh my God, their food is so fatty," she said, after picking up her menu and scanning the entrees. "I'm on a strict diet."

Of course, she was. I thought about Felicity eating lunch on the patio with me yesterday. It was refreshing to share a meal with a woman that didn't pick at her food or complain.

"Oh good, they have salmon," she finally said. "That's one of the few meats that I'm allowed to eat."

My stomach rolled at the thought of

smelling seafood, one of the few things that I didn't eat. *Ever.* But I was going to try and suck it up.

When the waitress returned with my old fashioned, I took a sip while Alicia ordered her food.

"I'll take a grilled salmon filet with a side salad. No dressing."

"Are you sure?" the waitress asked, writing on her notepad. "We have many fat free options if you'd like to hear them."

Alicia frowned. "Of course, I'm sure. Don't you know that even fat free dressing is bad for you? If you care about what you look like, you're willing to eat your vegetables plain."

"You're right," the waitress agreed instantly, and pasted on an apologetic smile. "I'm sorry about that."

I couldn't help thinking about Felicity as I watched Alicia treat the waitress so rudely. How many times did the other woman have to deal with snooty people that thought they could treat the waitress like crap just because they had money? I was willing to bet that she put up with their haughty behavior all the time.

When it was time to place my order, I made sure to be polite to the woman while Alicia turned her attention to the window, glancing left and right like she was looking for something.

"Anything interesting going on out there?" I asked after I'd ordered a steak and handed over both of our menus to the waitress. The woman hustled away, probably to deal with more ungrateful customers.

Alicia looked back at me with pursed lips. "No, not yet." She cleared her throat. "I mean, Charlotte's so dull, you know? I grew up here, so it's still my home for now, but after traveling to places like Milan and Paris, I want to live somewhere more exciting."

I disagreed with that completely. I had done a lot of traveling in my life, both vacations and work purposes, and I had seen some amazing places, but there was something about the city I'd lived in my entire life that just kept drawing me back here. I knew this place. It was comforting to have that kind of familiarity, to have a home.

Between the food choices and our differing views about Charlotte, I was starting to really question our compatibility. I didn't need a woman that was just like me, but if I was hoping to find someone to marry, we had to be able to find common ground.

This was the problem with dating and the reason that I had so little faith in Felicity's dating app. Finding a good match was complicated. If I was just planning to take Alicia to bed, I wouldn't care at all about what she ate or where she planned to live. It wouldn't matter. All that counted when hooking up was physical attractiveness, and she had that in spades.

But I wasn't going to give up on this date just yet. I had a feeling that Felicity would never let me hear the end of it if I didn't give this woman a fair shot, and I wouldn't want to be accused of purposely sabotaging her attempts to set me up with someone.

So, I listened as Alicia chattered on and on about places that she'd been, traveling all over the world for fashion shows and photo shoots. She peppered in plenty of bragging too, telling me about how much the other models hated her for being so attractive and winning all kinds of modeling jobs. She also made sure to mention all the men that wanted to be with her, seeming most proud as she detailed the creepy instances when a man started stalking her.

I tried to listen like I was interested, but I was finding her too shallow for my tastes. Still, when she finally switched around the topic, asking me about my job, I jumped at the chance to share the most important part of my life. I started telling her about the business opportunity I was considering with the motorcycle dealership, but she quickly jumped on that topic and brought up her crazy ex-boyfriend who fixed up old bikes for a living.

I tried to stifle my annoyance at her monopolizing the conversation yet again, talking about herself as she shared stories about the man making a scene in public on more than one occasion because he was jealous of the attention she got from men. It was funny how the more she talked about how beautiful she was, the less attractive she became to me.

When the food came, shit really hit the fan. All of a sudden, there were flashing white lights right outside the window where we were sitting. There were paparazzi pressed up against the glass, taking pictures and videos.

What the fuck? How did they know we were here?

I hadn't told anyone, so the only people that knew about this date other than myself were Felicity and Alicia. I considered Felicity for a moment. I could tell how important her company was to her. Would she have leaked this information just to get even more publicity for her app?

No. My gut told me that she wouldn't. If there was one thing I already knew about Felicity, it was that she had more integrity than that.

So, I focused my attention on my date, who was preening and striking poses for the camera. She even got up out of her chair and came around to my side of the table, throwing her arms around my neck as she stood behind me.

Anger swirled in my stomach, making me

lose my appetite, despite the big, juicy steak sitting in front of me. Alicia had to have leaked this to the paps. I didn't know if it was just some desperate play for attention or if she was trying to further her own career by using me to get her name out there even more, but I wasn't happy about it.

Then, she leaned down and planted a kiss on my cheek, and I was done. I wasn't a romantic man, by any means, but I didn't like that she was doing that just for the camera. It made me feel used in a way that was far too familiar. People were always after my money or looking to somehow use my status to benefit themselves. I was so damn sick of it.

Brushing her hands off my shoulder, I shoved my chair back, careful not to hit Alicia with it. The last thing I needed was for something like that to be caught on camera, even if it was an accident.

"I'm out of here," I mumbled, pulling my wallet out and grabbing three one hundred dollar bills. I hadn't paid attention to the cost of the meal, but I was sure that this would cover it. I tossed the cash onto the table along with my napkin.

"What are you doing?" Alicia shrieked, going from smiling and kissing me to furious in the span of less than a second.

I sighed. As if she hadn't already drawn enough attention just by arranging for the paparazzi to be here.

"This isn't a good match for me. I'm done," I said, turning my back and walking away. I didn't need to argue with her in front of a bunch of cameras.

"You can't just leave me here," she called out.

But she wasn't following me, so I took that as a good thing. Based on her reaction, I was betting that no man had ever rejected her before.

Well, beauty could only get you so far.

I was more let down by this disaster of a date than I would have expected. As I left the restaurant, I thought about Felicity and how sure she was that she could pull this off.

Well, her first attempt was a total failure. At this point, I couldn't imagine sleeping with that woman, much less marrying her.

All I could do was hope that Felicity's next choice turned out better.

Chapter Nine

Felicity

I wasn't expecting Jackson to come home anytime soon. It wasn't even nine o'clock yet, but when I heard the front door opening, I prayed that it was him and not someone breaking in. I was still on the couch, and even though my ankle felt much better, I doubted that I could run from an intruder. I muted the TV and listened.

"Felicity?"

I let out a breath I didn't realize I was holding until I heard Jackson's voice.

"In here," I called out.

"Good, you're right where I left you," he commented as he walked into the living room holding a pizza box.

"What the heck is that?" I asked. I knew from my time on staff that The Blue Ember had excellent food. "Didn't I send you out to a fancy restaurant?"

"Yeah, with a crazy lady," he said drily as he placed the box down on the coffee table.

I winced. "Crap, it didn't go well?"

"You could say that. She was rude to the waitress, talked about herself the whole time, and I'm pretty sure she invited the paparazzi to take pictures of us together."

Yep, that was bad. I had no indication that she was like that at all from her profile, but maybe I should've looked a little closer somehow. I hated that it was a failure. I'd been hoping to knock it out of the park on the first try.

But there was also a small part of me, buried deep down inside, that felt relieved. It was crazy, and I did the best I could to ignore the feeling or just push it away, but there was no denying its existence.

"I'm sorry," I said, not sure if he was angry or not. It was hard to read his expression. "I'll keep looking and find you someone great."

"We'll see," he said, one side of his mouth quirking up in a small half-grin.

I felt the tension leave my body. He wasn't upset.

I was still on the couch, sitting with my laptop on my lap. I had been catching up on work. The dating app was proving to be a success, but The Femme Code had produced eleven other apps in the past two years. They'd been moderately successful, but I believed we could do better. I was trying to research ways to get more traction for some of those apps before Jackson got home, but now, I pulled up ForeverLuv and started searching for another woman for him.

"Are you hungry?" Jackson asked, unbuttoning his suit jacket and tossing it onto his recliner before taking a seat on the couch beside me. He flipped open the square box, revealing the thin-crust pizza he'd brought home. It had peppers, mushrooms, and sausage.

"No, thank you. Drake made me dinner before he went home for the night."

It turned out that Drake worked from seven in the morning until seven in the evening, and then went home for the night. I thought those were long hours, but he'd informed me that he didn't work Monday or Tuesday. Jackson usually spent long hours at work during the week, so they'd decided this was the perfect schedule for Drake.

"Well, if you change your mind, I won't be able to eat the whole thing myself," he said.

I wrinkled my nose, making him chuckle.

"What?"

"Mushrooms, that's what."

He just shook his head, picked up a slice of pizza and took a big bite. He relaxed back on the couch beside me. "So, what are we watching?"

"Oh!" I picked up the remote and unmuted it, allowing the sound of a woman belting out a song that I didn't know. "This is my favorite singing competition show. The judges vote someone off every week and the winner gets to perform as the opening act for a popular band *and* they get a contract with a record label."

"She's good," he said after listening to the woman sing for a moment.

"Yeah, that's Nicole and she's a fan favorite, but I'm not so sure about her. Her voice is beautiful, but it's..." I struggled to find the right word, "...almost *too* controlled. I like a contestant named Denny. He gets into his songs, and his voice is raspy and full of emotion."

"You sound like you have a crush," he said, waggling his eyebrows.

I shoved his shoulder. "Not everything is about crushes and romance," I said. "I just like music, but I can't place this song. Do you know it?"

"It's an oldie. Magic Man by Heart," he said easily.

I looked at him questioningly.

"What? Can't I know things?"

"Are you a big Heart fan?" I asked curiously.

"Not exactly. And I think that song came out in the seventies. It was my mom's favorite band when I was a kid. She listened to their CDs in the car all the time."

As Jackson talked, I was struck by how unguarded he seemed at this moment. I hadn't realized it before now, but there was always a bit of a wall up around him, even in his home. But now, with the sun down and just the two of us hanging out together, it seemed like he was fully relaxed with me.

It also didn't escape my notice that this was the first time that he'd voluntarily told me anything about either of his parents. I wanted to push for more information, and not just because I was trying to play matchmaker. I just wanted to know more about him, for myself.

But I didn't ask. I was afraid it would ruin the mood. I didn't want him to clam up, or close himself off again. And I really liked this version of him. He wasn't bad company, but I reminded myself that one pleasant evening together didn't mean that I wanted to marry the guy. So, as we watched the show, making guesses about who the judges would vote off this week, I was also on my computer, going through a massive list of women to try to find a better match for him. She had to be out there.

I wasn't ready to give up yet.

When the show was over, he closed the pizza box and stood, going into the kitchen and coming back empty-handed.

"Can I ask you a question?" I asked.

"Go for it."

He didn't resume his seat beside me. Instead, he leaned against the wall with his arms folded across his chest.

"What do you look for in a woman physically?"

He didn't answer right away. Instead, he looked thoughtful as his eyes roamed over my face, then down my body. I felt goosebumps break out over my skin.

"I don't know," he finally answered.

"You don't know?" I repeated, frowning. "How can you not know?"

"I think that physical attraction isn't about things like hair color or body type or whatever kind of answer you're looking for. I think there's more to it than that. It's a spark.

It's chemistry. I don't have a type of woman that I look for. What I'm looking for is a woman that sets my blood on fire. One that makes my heart pound a little harder just by being near. A woman that I want to take as my own."

Take me. The words were on the tip of my tongue.

Even with so much space between us, I felt overwhelmed by him. The way he was looking at me, the words that he was using that I was sure described me. I wanted him so much that I was tempted to ignore all the reasons that I shouldn't give in to that particular temptation.

Then, my phone dinged with a text message, ruining the moment. I gritted my teeth together but looked away and glanced at the screen. It was Rose, checking in.

How are things with your future husband?

I rolled my eyes, a smile tugging at my lips.

"Who is it?" Jackson asked.

Was I imagining the possessive quality in Jackson's voice? I looked up at him and felt a twinge of disappointment as I saw that his guard was up again. I was tempted to tell him that it was none of his business who texted me, which was the absolute truth, but I didn't. Something about the rigidness in his body compelled me to be honest.

"My sister. She's been checking in every day. Honestly, I think she's a little worried that you might be some kind of psycho," I teased.

He smiled, but it wasn't as warm as before, and I sensed that our fun evening was coming to an end.

"Well, I'd better go to bed," he said, pushing off from the wall and starting to make his way across the room. "I have to be at the office early tomorrow."

"Okay. Well, goodnight."

I watched him walk out of the room, wondering what would have happened if Rose hadn't texted me. Would I have found the courage to say what was on my mind? That I wanted him to show me that I was the one that set his blood on fire and made his heart pound.

That I wanted him to take *me*.

I'd never know for sure because the moment had passed and as far as I knew, I was going to find the woman he'd marry any day now.

Chapter Ten

Jackson

I rubbed my eyes with the palm of my hand, leaning back in my office chair. I was busy working all morning and my eyes were tired from reading reports and focusing on computer screens. Still, when my computer made the light tinkling sound that indicated I had a new email, I sat up straight and clicked on the program. Seeing that it was from Felicity, I opened the message, unsurprised to find that it was about another date. The woman worked fast.

She'd sent a link to the profile of the woman, who wanted to meet for lunch. Clicking on it, I was greeted immediately with picture of a beautiful female, but she was different from the last one, not nearly as flashy. She had red, curly hair and green eyes. Her skin was pale and clear, and she had a dimple in one cheek when she smiled. In a way, her natural good looks reminded me of Felicity, which I found intriguing before I even started to read about her.

Her name was Amber Payne, and she was a doctor. I scanned her likes and interests, but didn't put much stock in all that. People could lie about that sort of thing, and having the same interest in TV shows or a shared hobby didn't necessarily mean we were compatible. We'd have to meet to determine that.

Going back to the email, I saw that Amber had an hour free for lunch at noon, so I emailed Felicity back, telling her to arrange the date and have Amber meet me at a diner just down the street. I appreciated what she was trying to do when she got me and Alicia into The Blue Ember, but the truth was that I hadn't eaten there in so long because I had simpler tastes. It wasn't about money, hardly anything was for me. It was about being in a comfortable space with good food.

Once that email was sent, I got out of my chair and left the office to stretch my legs. Going past my secretary's desk, I headed down the hall to the small break room where we kept the coffee pot and poured myself a full mug with just a splash of cream. I could have had my secretary, Allison, get it for me, but she had enough on her plate right now, trying to handle travel arrangements for special guests coming in from out of town for a charity gala I was throwing tomorrow night. And I liked to get out from behind the desk occasionally anyway.

I headed back to my office, stopping at Allison's desk on the way. "I'm going to take a long lunch today. About an hour or so."

"Okay, Mr. Goodman," she replied, barely looking up at me as she straightened some papers on her desk.

Allison was a one-of-a-kind woman. In her forties, she was a former army sergeant that retired from the service five years ago after an attack overseas left her with nerve damage in her leg. But she kept in amazing shape, and I was halfway certain that she could kick my ass if she felt the need to do so.

Outside of that, she ran my work life with an efficiency that couldn't be taught. She was a natural from the moment she walked into this office over four years ago. I was damn lucky to have her and I paid her a lot of money to make sure that she knew how much I appreciated her.

"I've made the arrangements at the Four Seasons for the representatives from the charity tomorrow night," she told me. "And the entertainment has confirmed that they will set everything up in the morning."

"Great," I said, sipping my coffee. It was still a little too hot, but I needed the caffeine boost.

"And what about you?" she asked, her eyes filled with curiosity. "Will you be bringing a date? I can arrange for a corsage to be delivered to you tomorrow."

I rubbed the back of my neck. I didn't even think about a date, but it would be best to bring one. This would be a highly publicized event, and I didn't want the attention to be on me just because I didn't have a woman on my arm when it should be focused on the charity.

"Yeah," I said. "I'll figure something out."

Maybe I could invite Amber if I hit it off with her at lunch. Going back into my office, I resumed work for the next hour, finally drafting an agreement for the motorcycle dealership I wanted to invest in and sending it over to them to review. When I stepped out of the office, Allison was typing on the computer, probably updating my schedule. I knew that taking a long lunch threw everything out of whack and she had to work harder to make up for it, but she wasn't the type to complain.

"You want me to bring you back a sandwich?" I asked, and she paused to glance up at me.

"Of course." She grinned. "You know I love their Reubens, but make sure they put the dressing on the side this time. I don't want soggy bread by the time you get back here."

A smile tugged the corner of my mouth. "You're awfully bossy, you know that?"

"And you're going to be late for your lunch date," she pointed out.

I didn't even ask her how she knew about it being a "date", probably a lucky guess. The woman knew me so well that sometimes I swore she was psychic.

Leaving the building, I walked a block down the street, not bothering to take the car for such a short trip. Mel's Place was the kind of diner that you'd see in movies. Black and white checkered floor, red vinyl seats along the counter and booths that lined the walls. There was an old-fashioned juke box in the corner and the waitresses wore blue dresses with white aprons.

"Afternoon, Jackson." I was greeted by Mel herself, a woman with poofy white hair that spent her time behind the main counter, expediting food orders and making milkshakes.

"Hi, Mel." I waved her way.

Spotting my date sitting at a booth already, I headed in her direction. She was looking around the restaurant with an impassive expression. Sliding into the booth across from her, I offered her an amicable smile.

"You must be Amber."

Her smile was even better in person, making her eyes light up. "I sure am, and there's no need to introduce yourself. I think just about everyone in the city knows who you are."

I nodded, trying not to let it show that that notion bothered me a little. It was so strange to be famous for nothing other than being rich and to constantly feel like the world has its eyes on you. I'd never liked it, but it was one of the few things in my life that I had no control over.

The waitress came over then, putting down a glass of sweet tea in front of me, my usual drink order.

"Hi, Jackson. How you doing today?" Most of the staff here knew me because I stopped in for lunch so often.

"Just fine. This is Amber," I said, gesturing to my lunch date. She was perusing the menu but looked up at the sound of her name.

"Welcome to Mel's Place. Can I get you a drink?"

"Uh...a chocolate shake, I guess."

It looked like Amber wasn't afraid to eat, which was another mark in the plus column for her. When the two of us were alone, I stayed quiet, giving her a moment to look over the menu. A creature of habit, I already knew what I wanted.

"So, why don't you tell me a little about yourself," I suggested when she closed the menu and put it aside.

"Well, I work at Angels of Mercy Hospital. I'm a resident."

Before we could get too far into the conversation, the waitress returned with the milkshake. Placing it on the table in front of Amber, along with a straw, she pulled out her order pad.

"You getting the usual, Jackson?" she asked, and I nodded.

"And a Reuben to-go for Allison when I leave. Dressing on the side."

She chuckled. "Trust me, I know. She gave me an earful last time. She's a spitfire, that one. And how about you honey?"

"I'll try a bacon cheeseburger," Amber said.

"That happens to be my regular," I told her when we were alone.

"So, you come here a lot? I'm surprised. I would think that a man like you would eat somewhere...*nicer*."

I glanced at the counter to make sure that Mel didn't hear that comment, but I didn't have to worry. She was talking to a man sitting on one of the stools.

"I like this place," I replied, and shrugged. "It's convenient to where I work and the food is good."

"Okay, I get it," she said with a nod that made her red curls bounce. "Work must take up a lot of your time."

"It does. But we all have to earn a living right?"

"Most of us."

I didn't know what she meant by that, and she didn't elaborate. We fell into a silence that quickly became uncomfortable. I wasn't sure how to break that awkward quiet. I was getting a strange vibe from her. Initially, she just seemed nice, but a few of the comments she made were getting under my skin. I checked the time, knowing that I had plenty of work to do this afternoon, so I needed to make sure that I wasn't gone longer than an hour.

"Is that a real Rolex?" Amber asked, and I felt my heart sink when I looked at her. I recognized that look in her eyes. It was a special kind of greed that was attracted to me. The kind that came from people that saw me as a walking dollar sign instead of a person.

"Yes," I said shortly.

The food arrived then, and I was glad that it cut off the conversation. I needed to think.

I was tempted to end the date right there, but I didn't want to cut it off prematurely just like last night. Telling myself not to jump to conclusions, that it was just a simple question, I tried to let it go.

"So, you're a doctor. Or...a resident. Tell me what that's like."

She sighed, resting her chin in her hand. "It's hard. Way harder than I thought it would be. To tell the truth, I'd love to quit, but I have so much medical debt..."

I knew where this was going. Still, I felt like I should test, just to be sure.

"You know, my dating profile doesn't mention it," I said nonchalantly, "but I'm actually hoping to find someone to marry. I'm looking to settle down very soon."

Amber's entire face lit up. "Me too! I think it'd be great to be married."

I took a bite of my burger and took my time chewing it while I watched her. I could practically see the excitement radiating off of her and as much as I wanted to believe it was for me, although that would also be strange because we just met, I knew in my heart that it was about my money.

"Of course," I continued when I swallowed my bite. "There's a lot to consider. The right person, the prenuptial agreement—"

"Wait, why do you need one of those?" She sounded way too offended for the topic of conversation.

"It's about protecting myself and my assets."

I didn't tell her that there would actually be a different agreement in place with the woman I married, one much like the contract I sent to Felicity, outlining the expectations and duration of the marriage and the amount of money that I would pay the woman after one year of marriage.

"But, it's so negative." She wrinkled her nose in displeasure. "It's saying that you don't trust the person you marry."

"It shouldn't be a problem if the woman I marry wants to be with me and not just to get her hands on my money."

At that, Amber's eyes narrowed and she left out a huff of air. "Well, good luck finding someone that wants to marry you with one of those."

The rest of the lunch was painfully awkward, with stilted small talk as we ate. We both knew the truth about her motives for coming to this lunch. She wanted to marry a rich man that would take care of her, allowing her to quit her job. I wasn't going to be that man. I was looking for an equal partner, not a kept woman.

When we were done eating, she didn't linger for long. Thanking me for meeting with her, she just took off while I paid the bill.

Feeling more disheartened than ever, I took Allison's sandwich and left the diner, walking back to the office slowly. It wasn't that I was disappointed about Amber, I barely knew her. It was just the same old story and I was sick of it. My entire life, it had been so hard for me to know if any of the people in my life gave a damn about me or if they just wanted to know me and kiss my ass because I was rich.

It was a lonely life and I couldn't stop thinking about it, even when I returned to work. It affected my concentration and that just irritated me more.

The day finally concluded at five. No more meetings or paperwork and Allison went home. But I didn't want to do the same. I wasn't in the mood to go home and face Felicity and tell her what happened on the date. She'd already texted and called me twice, but I didn't answer. It was so depressing that Amber just wanted my money that I didn't want to talk about it. Not yet.

So, I got in my car and drove to the bar. All I wanted to do was drown my troubles away with bourbon.

Chapter Eleven

Felicity

I nibbled on my bottom lip, telling myself that it was silly to worry about a grown man, but there didn't seem to be a way to turn it off. Jackson had been unreachable since his lunch date.

I assumed that it was because he was busy at work, but it was almost seven o'clock and he still wasn't home. Drake was off for the night, so I was left to do nothing but pace the floor and wait by myself.

Why didn't he just call me back? Shoot

off a text? Was it so hard to let me know that he was okay?

I knew that I was being crazy. I wasn't even his wife or girlfriend. He didn't owe me an explanation at all, but I couldn't help myself. I was restless and frustrated.

At least my ankle felt better.

Finally, I saw headlights coming up the driveway. I went to the front door and pulled it open as a black Porsche parked. It was unfamiliar to me, but when the passenger side door opened, Jackson stumbled out. From behind the steering wheel emerged a man that could only be his brother. They had a similar facial structure and the same kind of dark brown hair.

"You must be Felicity," he said, coming up the steps until he reached me.

"Yeah, and you're Chase, the family comedian," I said wryly. The one who'd signed Jackson up on ForeverLuv without his knowledge.

Chase's easy going grin showed that he wasn't a bit surprised to be called that. "Well, someone needs to try to get Chuckles over there to lighten up," he said, jerking his thumb in Jackson's direction.

Jackson was still too far away for me to see his face well, especially in the dark, but if his clumsy steps were any indication of his condition, I would say he was drunk.

"Piss off," Jackson shot back at Chase, his words just a little slurred.

"Language, brother," Chase admonished in a teasing voice. He turned back to me while Jackson approached, his gaze giving me a quick once-over. "You know, Jackson didn't mention that his matchmaker was so attractive."

There was charm dripping off this guy in spades and it was all directed at me. I just smiled and opened my mouth to speak when I was cut off by Jackson interrupting again.

"Hey!" he yelled out to Chase, who continued to look amused by the entire situation. "Back off, buddy. That's *my* back-up wife."

"Oh my god," I groaned, shaking my head. "You're ridiculous."

"No, I'm not," he retorted, his tone miffed. "I just need to make sure that I get married. It's the money...everybody cares so much about the fucking money."

He was close enough now that I could see that his eyes had that bleary look of someone who'd over imbibed. His rambling continued, stringing together words that didn't completely make sense, and he also smelled like some kind of strong alcohol.

"I'd better get him inside and into bed," Chase said, grabbing onto Jackson's upper arm as he led his swaying brother into the foyer. "He's gonna be miserable in the morning."

I had no doubt about that.

By the time I came downstairs for breakfast the next morning, Jackson was already in the kitchen, looking half-dead as he gripped a cup of coffee in both hands and sipped it slowly. It was Drake's day off again, so we were on our own for breakfast. I went to the refrigerator and grabbed some cream cheese spread. Then, I popped a bagel in the toaster.

Jackson winced at the small sound of the toaster being pushed down.

Yep, he was hungover. I had been there enough times to know that his head was probably killing him.

"How are you?" I asked, trying not to speak too loudly.

He just groaned and sipped his coffee again. His eyes were closed as he leaned on his elbows. When my bagel popped up out of the toaster, I added cream cheese and took a seat at the table near him.

"Okay, then tell me how the date went," I insisted when he didn't answer my first question. I was angry at him for not calling or texting me back yesterday to tell me what happened with his date, so I was going to get it from him now.

"I don't want to talk about it," he said. He sounded miserable, his voice hoarse.

"Too bad." I took a bite of my bagel and watched Jackson breath heavily.

"My head is fucking killing me."

I didn't have a response for that one, so I just waited for him to continue. I wasn't giving in.

He sighed and slanted me a glare. "Fine, I'll tell you how it went. You screwed up *again.*"

"What?" I gaped at him. What the hell was his problem now?

"You heard me. The date sucked," he snapped irritably. "She was a money-hungry gold digger. You should have seen the way she acted. It was so *obvious.* I can't believe that you haven't found a better option yet. The clock is ticking, you know. You're running out of time."

I bristled. "Don't you think I know that? It would help if you'd actually answer the phone and give me feedback when the date is over, you know. You can't just go running off to get hammered every time you have a bad date."

"You don't understand." He hesitated, his voice no longer cold and harsh. He just sounded...sad. "Sometimes, I need it. The alcohol helps erase the past. Helps me forget."

That cooled down my anger quickly. "What does that mean?" I asked.

"Nothing," he said, putting down his coffee cup and pushing back his chair.

He was about to make a run for it to avoid the conversation, but I wasn't going to let him do that. As he stood, I reached out and grabbed his wrist, holding him in place. His brown eyes locked on mine, and I could see that this was a painful conversation for him, but I felt like it was one that we needed to have.

"Damn it," he grumbled, sitting back down hard. "It's Natasha, my ex-fiancee. I don't like to think about her, okay?"

Whoah. That bit of information got my attention.

"Ex-fiancé?" So, he didn't always refuse to believe that love was real. He'd had it once and lost it somehow.

He pulled his eyes away from me, staring at the table, and I got the impression that he was ashamed.

"She said she loved me," he said, his voice rough. "Back in my college days. I was young and naive. She was lively and fun, so free with her life. She had me hook, line, and sinker. I was crazy about her."

"What happened?" I asked.

His smile was tainted by bitterness. "Same thing that happens all the fucking time. It turns out, I was nothing more than a bank account to her. She cheated on me, with multiple men, and when I caught her, she admitted it to me. Told me that she just wanted the kind of life my money would provide. She wanted to be treated *right*."

"So, when you went on the date with Amber, and she was all about your money..."

"It breathed new life into some old demons," he finished for me. "I just didn't want to remember those feelings. I was an idiot back then. I was blind and I let myself get hurt, and reliving that is a fucking nightmare."

I was getting my first glimpse of a new side of Jackson. A lonely, vulnerable side that completely contradicted the cool and cocky billionaire that he liked to present himself as. My heart hurt for him.

"You know what, let's take a break from the dates, just for tonight," I suggested.

It was already Tuesday, and I was feeling slightly panicked about finding someone, but

I couldn't imagine setting him up on another date right now. I needed to more thoroughly vet these women to make sure this didn't happen again. Because he was right, there were way too many people that were only interested in his money. It was sickening. There was a person beneath all that green, and I was starting to think that he was a good man, too. He deserved to be seen for more than just what he had in his bank account.

"I don't know," he said, scrubbing his hands down the scruff on his face. "I'm supposed to bring a date to this charity gala I'm throwing tonight. It'll look bad if I'm alone."

"I'll go with you."

The words slipped out of my mouth before I could stop them. I shouldn't do this, a voice in the back of my head made that very clear, but before I even got a chance to try to talk my way out of it, Jackson gave me a smile, his first real one of the morning. He looked so grateful and relieved that I knew I had to follow through. I was a woman of my word.

"You really want to?" he asked.

I nodded. I was just going to make him

look good, so that he'd have *someone* on his arm, I told myself. I wasn't sure that responsibility was mine to take on, but I was going to do it.

For Jackson.

Chapter Twelve

Jackson

I was waiting in the foyer for Felicity to come downstairs. The gala was just starting, so if we left now, we'd arrive at the perfect time. Fashionably late.

I was on the phone, talking to my father. I was trying to convince him to at least release a portion of my trust fund to the charity. I didn't just throw these events and pick the pockets of my guests. I contributed my own money as much as possible. But I was nervous about taking from what I made at my equity firm. I'd always had the trust fund to fall back on. Now, that was out of my reach, but my father could at least use some of my money to help people.

I was so wrapped up in our conversation that I didn't even see Felicity coming down the stairs until she was in the foyer, standing directly behind me. When I turned around and caught sight of her, my voice trailed off mid-sentence.

Jesus, she was *gorgeous*. There was no other way to describe her. The deep purple dress that she was wearing was low cut in the front, revealing lots of cleavage. The smooth white skin on display was begging for my touch, my mouth.

Her hair was down, and it was the first time I'd ever seen it like this. Dark brown waves fell halfway down her back, silky smooth and framing her beautiful face. She was wearing her glasses, but she also had makeup on for the first time since I met her. Smokey eye shadow and red lips. It wasn't much, and definitely wasn't necessary when she was already so pretty, but I liked it. She was so well-put-together and a part of me wanted to mess her up. To smear that lipstick with my own mouth and turn her hair into a wild mess by laying her on her back in my bed while sifting my fingers through those long, silky strands.

I cleared my throat and told my dad that I'd have to call him back before hanging up the phone. "You look amazing," I said. I couldn't seem to stop running my eyes all over her.

"Thanks," she said, looking down at the dress, which was the perfect length to barely brush the floor. "It's a bridesmaid dress from a wedding I was in a couple of years ago. When my business partner, Madison, got married. I've always held onto it, looking for an opportunity to wear it again."

I liked that she chose to wear this. Not only did she look stunning, but it meant something to me that she didn't ask me to buy her a new dress, which so many women would have insisted on. She wasn't using me for my money. In fact, she was a hard-working, independent woman. I admired that about her.

She'd already earned my respect.

"Should we go?" she asked, and I snapped out of my thoughts, offering her my arm. I led her out to the car, opening her door and getting a hell of a view down the front of her dress as she slid inside.

She caught me looking, and she blushed, her cheeks and neck turning a light pink color. There was something so damn appealing about that show of shyness, even as it contrasted with the sexy dress that showed off her body.

The gala was being held at the banquet hall of an upscale hotel. Parking in front, I blinked as lights flashed at me, reminding me of my disastrous date a few nights ago. But this was the press that I invited personally. They were covering the event because I'd learned over the years that when the fundraising events were in the news, the extra exposure usually resulted in an increase in donations in the days following the event. It wasn't just the wealthy elite that donated to a good cause.

Walking around to the other side of the car, I opened the door for Felicity, holding out my hand to help her stand. I had the strangest feeling as she slid her palm against mine and stepped out of the car, to my side. It was as if something significant was sliding into place, jolting me.

But this wasn't the time to evaluate that feeling or what it might mean. Stepping away from the car, I put an arm around her waist and waved to the paparazzi with my free hand. Felicity was tense, and when I turned to look at her, I could see that she was uncomfortable, despite her attempt to smile. I tightened my hold on her waist and tilted my head until my lips brushed the shell of her ear.

"Relax," I whispered. "They can smell fear."

Sudden laughter escaped her throat and all rigidity bled out of her. I still didn't loosen my hold on her though. This time we turned to the cameras together and her smile reached her eyes.

We didn't stay there for long, as there were other guests arriving. Heading into the building, we gave our names to a man at the door who checked them off on a list on an iPad. He held the door open for us and we walked into the already crowded ballroom.

There was a crystal chandelier hanging above our heads and white marble beneath our feet. The walls were red with golden trim, giving the space an elegant feeling. There was a small stage on the other end of the room where a string quartet was set up, playing arrangements of modern music while couples paired off and danced. There were tables with white tablecloths near where we were standing, and waiters in black and white uniforms were walking around with trays of champagne and hors d'oeuvres. I saw several familiar faces, but I didn't know everyone here, even though I was the one throwing this event. It didn't matter. All that I cared about was that they had deep pockets.

"You know, I can't believe I didn't ask this before, but what charity is this for?" Felicity asked.

"It's a foundation that does research on glioblastoma. Brain cancer. My dad's sister had it, and they were so close that it was a hard loss for all of us. Ever since she passed away, I've done at least one fundraising event a year for that cause."

"Oh, wow," she placed a comforting hand on my arm. "I'm so sorry."

"It was ten years ago," I said, but I appreciated the sentiment. Losing my Aunt Cathy had been tough, and I never forgot how hard it was on my dad.

"Are we going to dance?" Felicity asked, and I appreciated the change in subject.

I didn't like to share personal stuff like that with anyone, but I did find myself opening up to Felicity more and more. At first, I told myself it was because she needed to know me as well as she could to find a suitable wife, but now I was starting to think there was just something about her that made it easy to let her in, to allow her to see a deeper side of me. She was a good listener, but there was more to it than that.

Frankly, it was a little unnerving. I felt like this woman had come along out of nowhere and gotten under my skin in such a short period of time. It made me feel out of control of my life, and the most troubling part was that I liked it. As a man that put all of his focus on business and favored rationality over emotions, I was shocked to find that I liked the feeling of being swept away that I got when I was around her.

"Jackson?" She was looking at me with a furrowed brow, and I blinked, realizing that I'd been lost in thought and never responded to her question.

"I'm sorry, what did you say?"

"I asked if you wanted to dance?"

"Oh, Uh...no. I'm not a good dancer."

"You're not?" Her smile was teasing.

"Why is that surprising to you?"

"I don't know. I guess you just seem like the type that would know how to ballroom dance."

I chuckled. "Why? To impress women? Not exactly the top of my priority list."

"Good point," she said in a light-hearted tone.

A waiter was walking by, so I grabbed two champagne flutes off his tray and handed one over to my date. Then, I offered her my arm.

"How about we work the room instead?" I asked.

Felicity looped her arm through mine and I went about taking her around, introducing her to the men and women that I knew. There were CEOs, politicians, inventors, and other venture capitalists, like myself. Considering how high-profile most of them were, some people found them intimidating, but Felicity wasn't fazed. She didn't fawn over anyone or make a big deal about who they were, even the people that got more attention from the press than I did. She just made effortless conversation with everyone, especially if they were in the tech industry.

We ended up spending hours talking, not a dull moment arising. It occurred to me that I was usually bored at these events by now. And drunk. I didn't put the pieces together before, but now I thought that the reason I didn't usually enjoy these events more was because of the company I chose to keep. Most of my dates in the past were vapid. Nice to look at with a flat personality.

I hadn't purposefully chosen that type of woman, but it was probably because they were easy to get along with. When you're not looking for a serious, emotional connection, you don't want to put work into a single fundraiser date. But I liked the way Felicity was different, the way that she challenged me.

Who would have thought that her defiant sass would be so damn appealing?

"You're good at this," I said as the two of us walked toward the tables, planning to find a seat for her before I went up to the stage and made the obligatory give-us-money speech.

"Thanks." She grinned. "I'm actually having a lot of fun."

I took her empty champagne glass from her hand, her second one of the evening, and I put it on the empty tray of a passing waitress along with my own. We'd almost reached the tables when a couple approached us. I'd never met them in person before, but I knew who they were immediately.

"Mr. Goodman, it's nice to officially meet you," the woman said.

This was Amelia Harrington. She was the head of the foundation that we were here to support. I'd been donating money to them for years, so we'd had a lot of communication via email, but this was the first event that she'd attended, and she brought her husband, an oncologist that ran their research lab.

"Call me Jackson, please," I said, letting her pull me into a hug. "This is my friend, Felicity Wright. Felicity, this is Amelia and Paul Harrington. They represent the foundation."

"It's nice to meet you," Felicity said, shaking their hands.

"Jackson, you've done a wonderful job with all of this." Amelia gestured to our surroundings, beaming happily. "Every year, it seems like you bring in more and more money for the cause. You know, it's because of big donations like the ones we get from you that we're able to start clinical trials this fall on a new, experimental treatment. It's very promising."

"I'm glad to hear that," I replied.

"We were just going to go take a seat," Paul chimed in, putting his hand on his wife's back. I recognized the possessiveness in the gesture. "Would you like to join us?"

"I'm heading to the stage to make a speech, but I'll join you all afterward."

Amelia and Paul both nodded and headed to their seats while Felicity turned to me with a small smile. "Good luck."

I watched her walk over to the table and join the couple. They were strangers to her but that didn't hold her back. As I climbed the steps of the stage, I saw her chatting with them like they were old friends.

I was waiting for the quartet to finish their current song before taking the microphone, and as I stood there, it occurred to me that I had left something off my list of requirements for a bride. I liked the idea of having someone on my arm that I could trust to be friendly and sociable at events like this, someone that was smart enough to hold her own when I wasn't around.

Although, I was starting to think that the whole matchmaking thing was a bad idea. Did I really want to be paired up with some random woman off the street?

I wasn't so sure anymore. If the disastrous dates that I'd gone on so far were indication of what I had to look forward to for the rest of the week, I couldn't see how I would end up with the right match. But I respected Felicity too much to pull the plug now.

That respect was also part of the reason that I was starting to really hope she didn't succeed. Maybe it would just be better if she was forced to follow through on her hasty promise to marry me herself.

Yet, something about *that* thought didn't sit well with me, either. Despite how compatible *we* seemed to be, I really didn't want to force her to do anything.

The song ended, and I took the stage, stepping up to the microphone with my most charming smile on my face.

"Ladies and gentlemen, welcome to the sixth annual gala to benefit The Glioblastoma Research Foundation. I hope you all remembered to bring your wallets."

There was a smattering of light laughter. This could be the uncomfortable part of a fundraising event, the time to ask for money, but I found that the best way to get past any awkwardness was to lean into it. There was no point in pretending that we were here for any reason other than to collect donations.

My speech was well-rehearsed, and I delivered it flawlessly, pausing in all the right places to allow for laughter as I cracked witty jokes. The subject of brain cancer was intense, so I tried to lighten the mood. The more the guests enjoyed themselves, the more money they were willing to dish out. As I reached the end of the speech, Allison opened the doors at the entrance of the ballroom, allowing a group of ten people in red costumes to enter.

"And now, I present to you The Peacocks, the finest Chinese acrobatic group in the country."

While I spoke, they started their act, doing flips and tricks on the floor in front of the stage. There were cheers and applause as I left the podium, but I knew they weren't for me, and that was okay. The important thing was that everyone was properly entertained while Allison organized the collection of donations. She would go around with three other people and get pledges from every single person in the room. The woman really ran these events for me, and I reminded myself to give her another raise. She deserved it.

The rest of the evening seemed to fly by. Everyone was enamored with the acrobats and I found myself watching them with awe as well, even though I'd watched several videos of this group's performances before hiring them. It was just so much more impressive in person.

"You sure know how to throw a party," Felicity said, leaning closer to me to be heard over a final round of clapping when the acrobatic performance came to an end.

We were standing near the stage, where the quartet was finishing packing up their instruments. The crowd was starting to break up, with people saying their goodbyes and heading to the door. But all of that detail faded to the background for me as my eyes locked with Felicity's. She was so close and it was impossible to resist reaching out and brushing a strand of hair off her face, tucking it behind her ear.

Her dark hair was just as soft as I imagined, and when my fingertips brushed her cheekbones, her breath hitched and her eyes became dark pools of blue. To hell with it. I was going to kiss her. In this moment, I didn't care that it was a bad idea, or how it would complicate the matchmaking agreement that we had.

Consequences be damned.

I stepped closer, until there was only an inch of space separating us. Felicity's eyes widened, but she didn't back away. I knew that she was feeling this attraction, too. She tilted her head back, her lips parting, and I started to lower my face to hers...

Suddenly, a somebody bumped into Felicity from behind, jostling her enough to send her body tumbling into mine. My arms came around her waist to steady her, and I glared at the clumsy man that had knocked her off balance, not caring that he was a city councilman.

"Sorry about that," he mumbled, his speech slurred. He started to reach out to pat Felicity on the back, but seemed to think better of it when I pulled her tighter against me and ground my teeth together.

His wife took his arm, giving me an apologetic look and led the man away. But the moment was ruined and when I looked down at Felicity's face again, I could see that the desire had passed. She'd come to her senses, and I was just dealing with bitter disappointment.

What a way to end the evening.

Chapter Thirteen

Felicity

I needed to change my approach to this whole matchmaking thing. That realization came to me last night, after the gala. I was developing feelings for Jackson, and our almost-kiss had been a much needed wake-up call. I was getting in too deep.

It was his stupid idea to live together that was causing the problem. I liked being around him, seeing the softer side of the man. When we met last week, I believed he was nothing but a spoiled, pompous rich guy that was used to getting his way and happened to be hot as hell. Flashy window dressing with a cocky attitude. But spending time with him in his home, seeing him first thing in the morning and unwinding with him in the evening, showed me that he had depth. There was a softer side to the man, and that arrogant persona I saw the day we met was more like a mask, hiding the parts of himself that he didn't want others to see.

That was the reason I *liked* him.

It wasn't part of the plan.

I was only here to help my company, not get personally invested. Because Jackson might have proven that he was full of surprises, but there was one thing about him that held true from our first meeting; he didn't believe in love. He had no interest in a true romantic relationship with anybody.

That wasn't the kind of man I needed to be developing feelings for. It would be a sure way to get hurt. So, I needed to redouble my efforts to find him a woman to marry, because if I was stuck being his wife, I was bound to grow even more attached to a man that had made it very clear that he wouldn't ever feel the same way about me.

My new approach was going to involve a more thorough vetting of the potential matches. I had narrowed down the options to five women, and they'd all agreed to come meet me in person. I figured that was the best way to get a feel for who they really were. Dating profiles could only tell me so much, and I didn't want Jackson's next date to crash and burn like the others.

"I can't believe you're taking the afternoon off," Madison groaned from behind her computer screen. "There's too much work to be done for just two people to handle."

Christine didn't say anything, keeping her attention focused on her own computer, but the slight tick in her jaw told me that she was irritated as well. I felt like a jerk for not pulling my weight at the office, but they had to understand that this was all a part of the bigger picture. If I got Jackson hitched, he'd invest in The Femme Code as soon as his trust fund was available again. A little sacrifice now was worth it in the long run.

"I'm sorry, guys. I know this is a busy time for us—"

"Busy?" Madison interrupted. "ForeverLuv is a massive success, getting new members every day, and we're still trying to handle the influx of new clients. And you still need to call back that guy from the Morning Hour Talk Show that wants to interview you."

I rubbed my forehead tiredly. She was right, I had plenty to do.

"I'll call him on my cell phone and make the arrangements on my way to the coffee shop," I said.

"Coffee shop?" Christine finally joined the conversation. "Why are you going there? What does this have to do with your weird matchmaking deal with Jackson Goodman?"

I hadn't filled them in on all the details of that arrangement, since I signed an NDA, so they didn't even understand just how insane it really was. They thought I was just helping him find a girlfriend. My business partners had no idea that I was helping him find a wife to keep his trust fund—and if I failed, I was slated to be his *back-up wife*, as he'd told his brother. I wasn't sure if they'd approve or not, even if they knew that he'd promised to invest in our company.

"I'm having trouble finding a woman for him using the app, and the last thing we need is for him to delete his profile or, God forbid, go public with his *lack* of results." I pasted on a smile. "Do you want all this stress to go away?"

Christine sighed. "Fine, but you owe us."

"I'll bring in doughnuts tomorrow morning," I promised before walking out the door.

When I arrived at the small coffee shop that I had selected to meet the five women that I thought might impress Jackson, I saw my sister getting out of her car parked at the curb in front of the building. I had asked Rose to come along so that I would have some company, hoping that it might be less awkward to meet these strangers with her at my side. She was an easy choice since she was the only person that knew the truth about my agreement with Jackson, and the two of us hadn't spent much time together over the last couple of days.

I caught up with her at the door. "Thanks for coming."

"Why not? I love to play witness to a woman interviewing other women on behalf of a rich guy that wants to marry a stranger just so that he can stay insanely rich."

I grimaced. "Well, it sounds bad when you say it like that."

She just laughed as the two of us joined the queue for our coffees. The line was short and there weren't many people staying to enjoy their drinks. That was good. It meant that we were less likely to be overheard.

When we got to the counter, I ordered a mocha while Rose got an iced vanilla latte. I paid for both drinks since she was here doing me a favor. When we sat down at a table near the back of the dining room, I made sure that I could see the door. I knew what each of the women I was waiting for looked like, and the first one was due to arrive in fifteen minutes.

"So, how is it living with the dreamboat?" she asked.

I shrugged, trying not to let her see my conflicting emotions about the whole arrangement. "It turns out, he's not that bad once you get to know him."

"Really?" Rose arched a single eyebrow skeptically. "What happened to him being a 'smartass jerk that only has good-looks and a fat wallet going for him?'"

"Don't quote my own words back at me," I said, sticking my tongue out at her like a child. "Jackson has layers, believe it or not. There's a halfway decent guy under all that cocky swagger."

"Do I detect *affection* in your voice?" Rose asked with a know-it-all grin.

Damn it. She knew me way too well.

"What about you?" I asked in a blatantly obvious attempt to change the subject. "You told me you were seeing a man at yoga last week, but you didn't go into any detail. Who is he? How did you meet?"

"Um...we met at work actually."

I wasn't sure which was more concerning, the way that she fidgeted with the lid of her cup while avoiding eye contact or that she let me get away without answering her question about Jackson. We'd obviously stumbled onto a subject that made her uncomfortable, but that just piqued my interest. I wanted to know what she was hiding about this man.

"Is he a lawyer?"

Rose was a paralegal at one of the biggest law firms in Charlotte. Her bosses practiced criminal law, and the firm was one of the most sought-after options for anyone charged with a crime in the city.

"Yeah."

"Okay, spill," I said, waving a hand in the air between us. "What are you holding back?"

"Nothing," she replied a little too quickly.

"Then, what's his name?" I persisted.

"Jonathan."

These short answers were another sign that something was up. Rose was chatty, always had been.

"Does Jonathan have a last name?" I asked, picking up my mocha and taking a careful sip of the steaming liquid.

"Terrell. It's Jonathan Terrell."

I choked on my drink. Hot coffee scorched my throat as I hacked and a little even came out of my nose as I held a napkin to my face. It wasn't my most dignified moment, but I was too shocked by her words to care. Once I'd recovered from my coughing fit, I gaped at her.

"As in the law firm of Terrell, Daughtery, and Lowell? He's a partner?"

"Yeah, he is."

There was an almost defiant look in her eye now, and I already knew the answer to my next question before I even asked it.

"Aren't all the partners married?"

Rose chewed on her bottom lip and nodded.

"But he loves *me*," she was quick to add.

I couldn't hide my judgmental reaction. My face was too damn expressive, and she narrowed her eyes at me.

"Don't judge me, Felicity. You don't understand."

"No, I really don't," I agreed. That was one boundary I'd never cross.

"Not all relationships are perfect. I know you have this crazy romantic notion of finding the perfect man and living happily ever after, but that doesn't always work out so easily. But it doesn't matter. I love him so much."

"But you know you're doing something wrong," I insisted. "That's why you didn't want to tell me about him. He has a *wife*, Rose. Think about what you're doing to her."

"It's a loveless marriage," she shot back defensively. "Jon says that they haven't been happy in years."

A loveless marriage.

That was exactly what I had to look forward to if I didn't find a woman for Jackson soon. I'd probably end up in the same situation as Jonathan Terrell's wife, whether Jackson claimed we would be faithful to each other or not. It was easy to say that kind of thing when we made the agreement, but without an emotional commitment, there was no reason to think that he wouldn't be sleeping around while my one-sided feelings for him just got stronger.

The idea made me feel sick to my stomach. Even if we divorced after a year and walked away from the phony marriage as if nothing ever happened, I couldn't see myself getting out of it without hurt feelings.

"You know what?" Rose stood, putting her purse on her shoulder and picking up her iced coffee. "You can wipe that disgusted look off your face, because I don't need your approval. With your messed up situation with this crazy rich guy you might end up marrying, I don't think you're in any position to judge me."

With a huff, she spun on her heel and left the coffee shop. I hated that she was angry with me, but I just sat there and watched her go. There was no point in following her. She was too angry for us to have a productive conversation, and I couldn't see what good it would do anyway. I couldn't pretend that I approved of her dating a married man, so all I could do was wait for the fight to blow over and hope that the topic didn't come up again.

The door of the coffee shop opened again and a leggy blonde woman walked in, dressed more for a nightclub than an afternoon in a low-key coffee shop, with her short red dress that left little to the imagination. This was the first potential match that I was meeting, and I forced all thoughts of Rose and her married boyfriend out of my mind as she approached the table.

It was time to get to work. It was the only way to keep myself from ending up in a loveless marriage of my own.

Chapter Fourteen

Jackson

My day was long and stressful. Sometimes, people in my line of work simply threw money at a new company and hoped for the best, fully trusting the people that started the business to run it effectively. I was more hands-on. I liked to make sure that things were being run right, to my high standards, and that the money I invested was put to good use.

Today, I spent hours at a restaurant that I

invested in six months ago. Restaurants were a risky business to give money to, but I liked to take a chance every once in a while. Of course, that was before my trust fund was cut off. Nowadays, taking a loss would be a much bigger deal.

So, when I paid a visit to the restaurant and learned that instead of upgrading the kitchen equipment and expanding to add an outdoor seating area to allow more customers to be served on a nightly basis, the owner of the restaurant had redecorated the place in a gaudy theme and was in the process of buying a food truck to take the food on the road, opening up a whole new can of worms that the place wasn't equipped to handle, especially with all the additional permits needed and hoops to jump through. Not to mention the additional staff that would have to be hired. I was forced to step in and put my foot down, which didn't go over well with management.

Not that I cared. It was my money that they were spending, and while I was meant to be a silent partner, I was also heavily invested in making sure that the business was a success. Finally, things came to a head when I threatened to back out of the whole deal.

By the time I got home from work, I just wanted to sit on the couch with a strong drink in my hand and zone out in front of the TV. I was coming to enjoy my evenings with Felicity over the last few days. It felt like she'd been living with me for much longer than she had, and I was even growing used to the unexpected connection we had. I stepped inside the house and let out a little sigh. It was good to be home.

Handing over my briefcase to Drake, I shrugged out of my suit jacket and headed for the stairs, planning to go up to my room and change out my suit. I'd only made it halfway up when Felicity appeared at the top of the stairs. She smiled at me, and I had the thought that it was nice to come home to someone other than the butler that I paid to be here.

"There you are. I've sent you three text messages and an email today. I never heard back."

"Sorry, I wasn't at the office for most of the day. Is everything okay?"

"Of course. I just wanted to tell you about your next date. It's tonight."

"Tonight?" I repeated, and I could hear the exhaustion in my own voice. I wasn't in the mood to deal with another disaster today.

"Well, yeah. It's Wednesday. I only have a week, you know."

God, I didn't want to go, but I wasn't going to refuse. This was the whole point of her being here. The deal was that she would set me up on dates, and I would end up with a wife and my trust fund would be reinstated. I had to follow through, even if I didn't want to.

"Fine," I said. "I'll go. Let me just go get changed."

"Wear something casual," Felicity said, coming down the stairs. She stopped when she was about to pass me and reached out to put a hand on my arm, giving it a squeeze. "I really think you're going to like her."

My stomach felt like it was being squeezed by an iron fist, so I just nodded and pulled away as I continued up the stairs. Splashing a little cold water on my face, I told myself to buck up and give this date a chance. It didn't matter that I was mentally exhausted. I had to look at this as a job that needed to be done. I always put work first, after all.

This was no different. Just business.

Stripping out of my suit, I went into my closet and grabbed a sweater and a pair of jeans. Running my hand through my hair to brush it back off my face, I glanced in the mirror. I had a five o'clock shadow and I could use another haircut soon, but I decided that I was presentable enough. Going downstairs, I found Felicity in the kitchen, eating a quesadilla at the kitchen island and chatting with Drake as he washed the dishes he used while making it.

"That looks good," I said, glancing around to see if he'd made one for me.

"It is," Felicity said. "But don't worry, you're going to have a great dinner."

"Where are we going? You have connections at any other fancy restaurants?"

"Not quite. But I came up with a great

idea." Her eyes lit up. "You're going to take a cooking class."

"Really?" I asked incredulously, certain my aversion was written all over my face. I had never even considered doing such a thing.

"Yes, *really*," she mimicked back to me. "It'll be fun. And it won't hurt you to learn to cook something for yourself, you know."

"Okay, *mom*."

She slapped my arm hard, but there was a smile on her face. "I texted you the address. The class starts in twenty minutes."

"You want to give me any information about my date?"

"Her name is Parker Delano, and she's a travel journalist. She'll be waiting for you outside the building wearing a red scarf."

I exhaled a deep breath. "Okay, I'll see you when I get back."

I had the craziest urge to move closer and hug her goodbye, maybe plant a kiss on her cheek. I shook my head at myself. Playing house with this woman was changing me already.

But I had a feeling that it wasn't just

living with a woman that gave me that compulsion. It was *Felicity*. Again, I thought about last night and wished that I'd gotten a taste of her when I had the chance.

Without another word, I left the house, using my car's GPS system to guide me to the address that Felicity had given me. I parked in the lot in front of a brick building and got out, immediately spotting a woman leaning against the front of the establishment with a red scarf around her neck. Her head was tilted down since she was looking at her phone, but I could see enough of her face to know that she was very attractive.

Her curly hair was brown and her features delicate. She was short and thin, dressed in a pair of dark-washed jeans and a V-neck shirt that showed a hint of cleavage.

"Parker?" I asked when I reached her.

She looked up, her dark eyes meeting mine. A smile broke out on her face, showing off perfectly straight teeth.

"Yep, that's me." She held out her hand.

"I guess you already know that I'm Jackson."

"Of course. Should we go in? I think the class is about to start."

"Lead the way."

I made sure to hold the door open for her as she walked into the building, and I got the chance to appreciate the view from behind too. Those jeans were *tight*.

We walked into a huge kitchen with six stainless steel tables set up with ingredients and cooking equipment that I didn't recognize. There were already five other couples standing together, so Parker and I took the last empty space.

"Do you cook often?" I asked. I already had a good feeling about this woman. She had a calm energy and an easy smile. Felicity did a good job this time.

"Not at all," she admitted. "I'm on the road a lot, staying in hotels and going out to eat at local restaurants so that I can include it in my pieces for the magazine."

I hadn't considered marrying a woman that travelled for work, but it sounded like a good idea. She wouldn't have to be a perfect match. I just needed her to agree to a marriage of convenience and our lives would barely have to change.

As the cooking class started, we made small talk. I told her about my job, and the importance of my time spent there. She shared her passion for traveling and how much she enjoyed being a writer.

It was a pleasant date, a good match. I wanted to believe that this was it, the woman that I needed. But something was missing.

It took me a while to realize what it was. It didn't come to me until we were halfway through making cheese ravioli from scratch. I handed Parker a spoon to stir the filling together, and our fingers brushed.

There was no reaction. She was pretty, with a body that I could appreciate, but the spark that I felt with Felicity wasn't there. I was sure that I could sleep with Parker if I wanted to and enjoy it, but that burning hunger that I felt for Felicity whenever I looked at her, the chemistry that made my breath hitch when we touched, wasn't present.

A week ago, I wouldn't have cared about such a thing. I didn't even know what I was missing. Now, I was growing addicted to that feeling of scorching desire, that flare of undeniable, mutual attraction, and I wanted to feel it for my soon-to-be wife.

"Oh my God, this is delicious," Parker said when the ravioli was finished and we were trying our food. "This pesto sauce you made might be one of the best things I've ever tasted."

"What can I say?" I quipped. "I'm a boss at reading a recipe."

Her laugh was light and airy.

"Well, I can't help but wonder what else you're good at." There was no mistaking the suggestive look in her eyes.

The class ended then as we finished our meal and everyone cleaned up. It didn't take long with the industrial dishwasher in the corner of the room. I walked Parker outside, and we headed to her car. It was a big Jeep, not what I expected from a tiny woman like this, but I figured that it fit her traveling lifestyle.

She was parked near me, and I saw her eyeing my car. "You know, this has been really fun. Isn't it a shame to end it so soon?

You know, you could follow me to my place..."

I hesitated. I knew that I should do it. If I took her up on her offer, it would undoubtedly lead to sex, and then I would know pretty much everything that I needed to about us being compatible. But when I didn't answer right away, Parker got impatient. Stepping into my body, she popped up onto her toes and pressed a kiss to my lips.

Again, I waited to feel a tingling warmth or a magnetic pull, anything close to the reaction that I got from Felicity's simplest touch. But it just wasn't there.

Parker was bold, which I liked. And seemingly normal. On paper, she appeared to be perfect wife material, but I found myself taking a small step back.

"Sorry, I'd better get home," I mumbled awkwardly, because what guy in their right mind refused such a tantalizing offer? "I have work in the morning. But I had a great time too."

Parker looked disappointed, but she nodded and turned to her car. I hated to let her down, which wasn't something that I was usually worried about when it came to women. Maybe that was just another way that Felicity was changing me.

Getting into my own car, I started it up and headed home. I wasn't sure what I was going to tell Felicity about how it went with Parker. I didn't want to see more disappointment in a woman's eyes tonight.

Chapter Fifteen

Felicity

I was in my room, watching videos on my computer of The Morning Hour Talk Show to prepare for next week's speaking engagement to talk about the massive success of ForeverLuv. I couldn't help wondering if I was going to tell them that Jackson Goodman had found his fiancé using the app. At this point, I had lost a little faith in my ability to find the right woman for him.

Maybe Parker was the one.

It was just after nine o'clock, and I found myself listening to see if I could hear the front door opening. What if he didn't come home at all? I didn't think I would be able to sleep a wink thinking about him in her bed.

No. This is what you wanted.

Yeah, that was what I tried to convince myself. But I couldn't seem to shake this anxious feeling that this whole thing was just *wrong*. I didn't feel good about it at all.

So instead, I tried to take a page out of Jackson's book and listen to my head instead of paying so much attention to my emotions. My head knew the score. The sooner Jackson found his bride, the sooner I could go back to my real life and forget all about my feelings for him.

My heart skipped a beat when I heard the front door of the house open. He was here.

Pausing the video on my laptop, I moved off the bed. I was in my pajamas, a navy-blue tank top with matching pants, but I didn't care about that. My body was completely covered. So, I stepped out of the bedroom, the hardwood floor cool under my bare feet.

Just like earlier today, I looked down the

staircase to see Jackson coming up. He looked tense, and I braced myself to hear bad news. How could the date not have gone well? Parker ticked off all his boxes.

"How was it?" I asked anxiously. "Did you like her?"

Are you going to marry her? I wasn't sure why I didn't ask that last question.

"It was fine," he said, moving past me and going down the hall toward his bedroom. Normally, I wouldn't follow him into his personal space, but I wanted to know what happened.

"What does that mean?" I insisted. "*Fine*?"

"It means what I said," he replied, his tone almost . . . flat. "No drama like the first two dates you sent me on. We cooked, we talked, and I came home."

He reached his bedroom and went inside, leaving the door open. I took that as an invitation to follow, but I lingered in the doorway.

"Are you going to see her again?" I shifted on my feet, wishing I could read him better. "Do you think I made a good match?"

"Sure," he said, his back to me as he walked to his dresser.

I watched him take his keys, phone, and wallet out of his pockets and put them on the dresser, waiting for him to tell me more. When he didn't, frustration bubbled up to the surface. I moved further into the room, grabbing his shoulder and turning him around so he had no choice but to face me.

"Talk to me Jackson." I searched his gaze and found . . . nothing. "What went wrong with the date?"

"Nothing," he suddenly snapped, moving away from me as he paced the floor. "Nothing at all except..."

"Except *what*?" I nearly yelled.

"I just wasn't feeling it, okay?" he said irritably. "There was no chemistry between us."

"Chemistry?" I felt like a parrot, just repeating everything he said. My voice got louder and louder as we continued this conversation. "Who cares about chemistry? You just need someone to call your wife for appearances' sake."

"I don't know what to tell you." His voice

was cool, the sharp contrast to my burning anger just making me more agitated than I already was.

"You could tell me why you're being so difficult," I said, jamming my hands on my hips. "So damn picky about a woman that you're not going to care about anyway."

His lips flattened into a thin line. "Yeah, well, maybe you just can't accept that you were too cocky when you agreed to this arrangement. *You* set the limit of one week, remember? It's not my fault that your time's almost up and you haven't found me a suitable match yet."

I marched right up to him, standing toe to toe. "Maybe there is no match for you," I snapped, my irritation spilling over. "I'm starting to think that no one on the planet can meet your high standards."

"Maybe *you* can," he mumbled.

I felt like my heart stopped as I stared at him, my anger melting away as if it never even existed while I tried to wrap my head around what he just said.

"Wha—"

I didn't even get the word all the way out

before Jackson's arms shot out, seizing me and pulling my body flush against his. Grabbing a fistful of my hair, he tugged just enough to make me tilt my head back and pressed his lips to mine in a heated kiss.

My thoughts became a jumbled mess as a desperate need took a hold of me. My lips molded to his, and I felt a shiver run down my spine as he reached around behind me with his free hand and cupped my ass. The kiss was rough, and I felt like he was laying a claim on me, branding me in some way that made my heart race wildly.

I gripped the back of his neck, gasping as he slipped his tongue inside my mouth. The taste of him was like an aphrodisiac throughout my system, and I moaned shamelessly. The next thing I knew, he was moving us, guiding me to the bed, his hands on my back controlling me as I was laid out flat on the mattress. Then, he was on top of me, his hands everywhere, stroking my neck, tracing the curve of my hips, and sliding up my shirt to palm my bare breasts.

I felt like a blooming flower, opening myself up to a pleasure that I had been trying so hard to deny. With his hands on my skin and his tongue dominating my mouth, I didn't care about the reasons that I shouldn't do this. None of that mattered. All that I could focus on was the pulsing ache between my legs.

I parted my thighs and he moved into the space, grinding himself against my core. My thin pajama pants offered no resistance to the hard, thick bulge in his pants, and I broke the kiss, sucking in a sharp breath of air.

"*Jackson...*"

His name was a desperate plea for more, and I knew he understood that as he started to kiss down the side of my neck, then along my collarbone, nipping the skin lightly. His hips undulated more slowly, and the sensation drove me crazy. I wrapped my legs around his waist, trying to give my swollen clit the friction it needed.

God, I'd never been so hot for a man.

Luckily, Jackson wasn't wasting any time. Rearing back, his hands found the hem of my tank top and he pulled it over my head, tossing it aside and leaving the top half of my body completely exposed to his heated gaze.

I wasn't wearing a bra, and my nipples

grew rock-hard in the cool air of the room. The sight of them made Jackson flash a wolfish grin before he lowered his head to my chest, taking a sensitive bud into his mouth and flicking it with his tongue before giving the other one the same delightful treatment. My back arched and goosebumps broke out all over my exposed flesh.

"You taste so fucking sweet, just like I knew you would," he murmured against my skin, and I realized that I wanted to see more of him, to kiss and touch every inch of his smooth, muscled flesh.

His sweater needed to go. I gripped it at his back, my movements clumsy and rough as I tried to get it up over his head. Urgency had taken over. I didn't want this to be slow and sweet, not after waiting so long for it. My body demanded more than that. I wanted him to unleash the passion I could sense just beneath the surface.

Smirking, Jackson helped me pull the sweater off, revealing his firm, lean torso. I'd seen it before when he was swimming, but it was different now. I wasn't admiring him from afar, like some creeper. Without restraint, I could trace the divots between his ab muscles with my fingertips, press my lips to his broad chest, and slid my tongue over a rigid nipple.

But Jackson didn't give me freedom to explore his body for long. His hand found its way into the front of my pants. His fingers dipped deep between my legs, sinking into my slick pussy, and he let out a tortured groan.

"*Fuck,* Felicity. You're so wet, baby."

"I know," I said breathlessly as his thumb found my clit and started moving in a tight circle. Shockwaves of raw pleasure radiated through me. "That's what you do to me. Every time you're near, my panties are soaked."

He laughed, low and dirty. "You naughty girl."

The way he said that just made me even hotter. Everything about this was wrong, but God, it felt so right and I couldn't stop.

The next thing I knew, Jackson stood from the bed just long enough to remove his jeans and boxers. My eyes widened at the sight of his erection jutting out from his hips.

He was bigger than any man I'd ever been with, long and thick. I subconsciously licked my lips, and he groaned deep in his throat.

"Lose the pants," he commanded, opening up the top drawer of his dresser and pulling out a condom. "Because I can't wait another minute to fuck you."

He didn't have to tell me twice. Shimmying out of my pajama pants, I watched, transfixed, as he rolled the condom down the length of his straining cock. Then, he joined me on the bed again, positioning himself between my spread legs. I pulled him down for another kiss, and he swirled his tongue inside of my mouth as he lined himself up at my entrance, the head of his shaft already pushing me open.

I tensed up, I couldn't help it. As much as I wanted this, I was also intimidated by his size. He ended the kiss to look down into my eyes. I was shocked by the tenderness I saw there. No smirk or stoic expression. Just earnest warmth and desire that made my heart swell inside of my chest.

"Relax," he murmured huskily. "I promise you'll enjoy it."

I nodded, forcing the rigidity out of my body as the blunt tip of him continued pressing into me. I let out a small gasp as the broad head slid inside, stretching me wide. Sweat broke out on Jackson's forehead as he pushed forward, inch-by-inch, giving me plenty of time to adjust to his size. When he'd finally bottomed out, I'd never felt so full.

And I wanted more.

Jackson paused, quivering as he hovered over me. I looked up to see that his brown eyes were so dark that they looked almost black in the low light coming from the bedside lamp. He was the picture of erotic male perfection with his arm muscles straining from holding him up, his lips parted to allow his ragged breaths to escape, and his thick hair falling roguishly across his forehead.

When I was ready for him to move, I relaxed and he took the hint. Withdrawing almost all the way out, he thrust forward again, drawing a cry of pleasure from my lips. I held onto his shoulders as he rocked against me, increasing his speed. . . faster . . . harder. . . until he was pounding me into the mattress, and I loved every second of it. A delicious pressure built in my core every time he drove himself deep into my body.

Fire raced through my veins and as my release rose up inside of me, I couldn't stop moaning in pleasure. The headboard of Jackson's bed banged against the wall as his movements became frantic, his thrusts short and rough. Then, he lifted one of my legs up onto his shoulder, and the angle of my hips allowed him to go even deeper, while his cock rubbed against a sensitive spot inside me that completely unraveled me.

I only lasted two more thrusts before my orgasm shattered my world. I bucked and shuddered as he kept thrusting through my climax and I cried out his name. Jackson's hands captured my own, intertwining our fingers and pinning them above my head as he found his own release, his body heaving hard against mine and his breath leaving him in a rush.

Our eyes met, and he muttered something that I didn't quite catch. The word "perfect" stuck out to me, but I was still riding the high of my orgasm, so I wasn't sure.

All I knew was that I'd just had the best sex of my life.

As we both came back down to earth, I knew that I was going to regret this tomorrow. But for tonight, I didn't have the energy to deal with the ramifications. I just wanted to enjoy this moment with Jackson while I could. So, I let him cover us with his blankets and I rolled onto my side, burrowing my face against the pillow.

He pulled me into his arms. Cocooned against his chest and the warmth of his body, and feeling more content than I could ever remember being, I let my eyelids flutter closed. My last thought before sleep took me was that being Jackson's wife would mean I'd get to fall asleep like this every night.

But only for a year.

There was no moment of disorientation when I woke up in the morning, no jolt of surprise when I realized I was sharing a bed with Jackson. Everything that happened last night was fresh in my mind the moment I came into consciousness.

I slept with Jackson last night.

Holy crap, we actually did it. My body was sore in the most delicious way, and I felt a small smile flicker across my face as my mind replayed the reason that I felt this way. Jackson was dominant in bed, as I'd expected, but there was also a tenderness that melted my heart. The way he looked at me...the way he waited until my body was ready before he started taking me hard...the feeling of his arms wrapped around me from behind all night long, my back pressed into his chest. Everything about last night had been total bliss.

Don't forget what this is.

The little voice in the back of my head was right. One night of fantastic sex and cuddling didn't change anything. Jackson still hated romance, and I still believed in love. Regret washed over me. No matter how good we were together, it wasn't worth getting my heart shattered, and I felt stupid for allowing anything to happen between us because I knew the facts of the situation beforehand. I just let myself get carried away. The moment he kissed me, I was a goner. The chemistry and sexual tension that had been building between us since the very first day we'd met had been too hot to resist.

Now, I just needed space, to give myself a chance to think with a clear head. Slowly, I lifted his arm that was draped across my waist and started to slide out of his hold. I had almost reached the edge of the bed when Jackson's arms tightened around me, pulling me back into him. Turning in his hold, I looked into his face, his half-lidded eyes sleepy.

"Where do you think you're going?" He asked playfully.

"I didn't know you were awake," I replied, biting my lip. I wanted to get out of his bedroom before he had the chance to stop me, but that wasn't possible now.

"I'm a light sleeper. And I'm not used to sleeping with another person."

"Me either." I swallowed hard. "Listen, Jackson, I think we should talk about what happened last night."

His smile disappeared. "Why do I have

the feeling that I'm not going to like this conversation?"

"It was a mistake," I said, cutting to the chase.

He loosened his hold on me, sitting up in bed with the blankets pooled around his waist. "What are you talking about?"

I sat up too, clutching the sheet to my chest. I wasn't exactly modest after what we did last night, but the way the conversation was going made me want to feel less vulnerable. I was already missing the warmth of his body.

"Come on, Jackson. You know that we shouldn't have slept together. It only complicates things."

He frowned, and I immediately felt guilty, although I wasn't sure why. I was just telling him what we both knew. But then I saw it, the hurt in his eyes. It floored me, but before I could say another word, he looked away and got out of the bed. I saw a flash of his naked backside before he was pulling on a pair of sweats he picked up off the floor. When he turned back around to look at me, I felt like I was staring at a stranger, his walls back up. His expression was remote and he shrugged his shoulders carelessly, the gesture a complete contrast to the emotion I'd just seen in his eyes.

"It only complicates things if you let it," he said dismissively. "I think you were a great fuck, really, and we both got what we needed, but there's no reason for you to freak out about it."

I knew that I'd initiated this conversation, but that didn't stop his cold words from stinging. They lashed at my heart, and I wanted to get out of this room more than ever. Things had taken an ugly turn so quickly and all I wanted was to go back to that moment of contented happiness I felt as soon as I opened my eyes.

Or better yet, go back to last night to relive the whole thing over again.

But neither of those were an option. So I pulled at the flat sheet until it was loose enough to gather completely around me. Getting out of the bed, I held it tight to my body as I scooped up my clothing from the floor. I could feel Jackson's eyes on me, but I didn't look in his direction again. In fact, I didn't even say another word. I was too worried that my vulnerable emotions would come through in my voice, and I didn't want him to know that I was devastated by the casual attitude he was showing about our night together. He was able to act like it was nothing so easily, and it would just humiliate me further to let him see that I wasn't able to do the same.

Sure, I said it was a mistake, but it was for this very reason. Jackson didn't have the same feelings as me. Or if he did, he was so good at burying them that I had no way of knowing if we were truly on the same page. It was enough to drive me crazy and definitely a good reason to label sleeping together as a lapse of judgement.

So, I walked out of the room with the sheet on my body and my clothes in my hand, trying to hold on to every bit of dignity that I had left as I did my walk of shame down the hall.

Chapter Sixteen

Jackson

I watched Felicity walk out of the room, my eyes transfixed on the tattoo of a blue butterfly on her right shoulder blade. I had no idea that she had one, and it was sexy as hell. But I couldn't focus on that right now. I felt like too much of an asshole.

I knew that I was acting like a jerk, dismissing our night together as nothing but a meaningless way to get off when it was actually the most connected I'd felt to a woman. *Ever.*

I was just upset to hear her say it was a mistake, hurt in a way I never thought possible, but I knew she had good reasons for thinking that way. Hell, I'd demonstrated to her that I wasn't the best guy to form any sort of attachment to.

But it didn't feel like a mistake to me. It felt right. Felicity was stirring up an overwhelming affection that I hadn't felt since Natasha broke off our wedding, shattering my heart and my trust in all women.

That was my other problem. These feelings I had for Felicity shook me. I liked to pride myself on being a fearless, ruthless businessman, but the way my heart stuttered when I looked into her eyes last night, then first thing this morning...that scared the shit out of me.

It was because I couldn't trust her, not completely. I had learned that lesson the hard way in the past. Also, Felicity had only agreed to our crazy arrangement when I dangled big investment money in front of her face. She could be just like Natasha.

Something inside of me rebelled at that idea, but I couldn't help thinking it. Felicity didn't seem like my ex and looking back at my relationship with her, I could identify signs that Natasha was using me, things that I overlooked. There had been no signs that Felicity was trying to do the same thing, but maybe she was just more cunning than Natasha. I couldn't be sure.

So, I told myself that I wasn't really falling for Felicity. We were a good match, and the sex was out of this world, but that was it. There was nothing deeper. Definitely not the bullshit concept of "love."

Going to my closet, I picked out my clothes for the workday and made a mental note to ask Drake to change my sheets today. The last thing I needed was the scent of Felicity lingering in my bed, heating my blood and driving me to do something stupid, like attempt to seduce her again.

Wouldn't want to make any more *mistakes*.

I was heading to the bathroom to shower when something pink and lacy on the floor caught my eye. I stopped and picked it up, feeling my cock stir as I realized it was Felicity's panties. I had been so eager to get inside of her that I didn't take time to appreciate her in them. Now, I wished I had. In fact, I should have taken the time to explore every inch of her with my mouth. I wanted to know what it felt like to have her come on my face, licking up her sweetness...

Fuck. Now I had a raging erection and no good outlet for it. Masturbating wasn't going to be nearly as satisfying as going down the hall to Felicity's room would be. But that wasn't going to happen. I just needed to get ready for the day and act like last night never happened.

But before I went to the bathroom, I opened my top drawer and tossed Felicity's panties inside. If this was a one-time thing, I was at least going to keep a souvenir.

Chapter Seventeen

Felicity

I had left Jackson's house early this morning, eager to avoid running into him in the kitchen after the awkwardness in his bedroom. I needed a little distance to get over my hurt feelings and get my head back on straight.

Leaving early turned out to be a good thing because I had time to stop and get the doughnuts that I promised Christine and Madison. By the time they both arrived at work, I was already behind my computer screen with a half-eaten cruller in my hand.

"Wow, look at you, hard at it," Madison said, grabbing a glazed doughnut from the box while Christine handed out the coffees she brought in.

"I told you that I'd make it up to you for leaving early yesterday," I said, turning around one of my computer monitors to show her what was on the screen. "I've been working on updates for some of our older apps. Have you seen the puzzle app we came out with a year ago has a sudden spike in downloads?"

"Yeah, can you believe that? We almost pulled it from the market and all it needed was for the company to have a boost in popularity."

"Well, I'm updating it with new images. It'll be done this afternoon."

"And what about the dating app?" Christine asked. She took a bite out of a jelly doughnut, making the filling come out the other end and land on her shirt. "Damn it..."

I couldn't help chuckling before I answered her question.

"We're still getting new downloads every day, and if you look at Tech World Magazine's most recent online issue, you'll see it on their list of Top Twenty New Apps Worth Downloading."

"Oh my God, are you serious?" Madison hurried to her own computer and started typing away, probably looking it up for herself.

This had been the busiest week The Femme Code had ever had, and I loved it. It was stressful, but in a way that made me feel like I was accomplishing something. We weren't fighting an uphill battle anymore, trying to stand out in an already over-saturated industry. We'd finally managed to do it.

But I knew that this success could be fickle. It all hinged on our dating app for now, but that wouldn't last forever. We needed to be a part of the next big trend too. And the one after that. And the one after that...

To stay on top, we needed capital. Which meant that I needed to follow through on my plan to find Jackson a wife. The thought of it made me feel queasy after last night, but I was just stubborn enough to try to power through anyway.

It was Thursday, so I was running out of time. According to the papers that I signed last week—which felt like a million years ago I would have to participate in a civil ceremony at the courthouse if I didn't fulfill my obligation to find him a bride by Sunday. Despite everything I was feeling, I didn't want that to happen.

In the early afternoon, I managed to carve out some time for perusing the app, trying to see if any of Jackson's matches on there looked like they had potential. It didn't take long before I realized that I couldn't pick one. I kept making up excuses in my head that would discount even the most perfect women. I didn't want to find her anymore. Everything had changed for me after last night, whether I liked it or not. I couldn't play matchmaker any longer, and I wasn't sure what that meant for the future of my company.

* * *

I purposefully worked late, staying almost an hour after Madison and Christine had gone home for the day. I was trying to avoid Jackson, not sure if I'd arrive at his house and find the interesting and funny man that I had been getting to know over the last few days or the closed-off stranger that he turned into when he didn't want to let me in.

I even considered going home to my parents' place instead of his house, but all my stuff was there. I had to face him. I just wished that I could save face and make him believe that what happened between us didn't mean anything to me either, but the only way I could think to do that was to give him the name of his next match, and I had nothing.

I was bracing myself for some awkwardness as I walked through the front door, but to my surprise, that wasn't what I encountered at all. Jackson must have seen my car pull into the driveway because he was standing in the foyer with his hands in his pockets, leaning against the wall like he didn't have a care in the world. Obviously waiting for me.

"Uh...hi," I said, pausing just inside the

door. His expression was unreadable, and I had to wonder if he was going to kick me out of the house. Maybe that would be for the best.

"You're later than usual. Have you eaten?"

His question was so unexpected that it startled an answer out of me.

"No."

"Good." He straightened from the wall and walked toward me. His movements were graceful and I felt like prey being stalked. "I want to take you out to dinner."

What?

Confusion spilled through me. After our disastrous morning-after, this was the last thing I expected, but I wasn't going to argue against it. Partially because I was starving, but I also just enjoyed being around this man, and sharing a meal with him sounded like a good way to spend my evening—instead of being alone with him for hours in this house. As long as we didn't discuss what happened last night, we should be able to have a nice time.

"Where?" I asked, wondering if I should

change into a nice dress. I was wearing skinny jeans and a red blouse that showed off my curves.

"It's casual," Jackson said, as if he read my mind. "A steakhouse."

My next question was about whether or not this was a date, but I decided not to ask him that. I didn't want to label a simple meal with a business associate especially if I wouldn't like the answer.

I followed him back outside, and he pulled open the passenger door of his Jaguar for me. I got inside, checking out the red leather interior. The console and dash were black with chrome accents and the vehicle had that new car smell that could be bought on an air freshener to hang from the mirror, but I was sure that it was legit in this case.

When Jackson got inside and started up the car, the engine purred and it ran so quietly that I could barely hear a thing. The dashboard lit up with light, and when he pulled out of the driveway, I couldn't believe how smooth the ride was. I wasn't much of a car person, but I could tell I was in a top-of-the-line vehicle and was adequately impressed.

It didn't take long to get to the restaurant, and I was enjoying the ride so much that we barely spoke a word on the way. That was okay with me. The silence wasn't thick with tension as I feared it would be.

The steakhouse was casual, just as he'd described, the kind of place that I would go myself. That was something else that I liked about Jackson. He had expensive cars and imported Italian suits, but he also knew how to appreciate things that didn't come with a massive price tag. Like a good steak.

The parking lot was packed, so we ended up at the back of the lot, which was surrounded by trees. I got out of the car before he got the chance to come around and open my door, but he shut it for me, and took my hand. Electricity danced up my arm at the contact, and the feeling was somehow comforting. The chemistry—as he called it—was still there between us. Sex didn't ruin it or the messed-up way that we both seemed to reject each other this morning.

Our fingers were interlaced, and Jackson

led me across the parking lot. The smell of cooking meat was thick in the air, even outside, and I felt my stomach rumble. Jackson must have heard it too, because he gave me a teasing grin and I felt myself flush. He pulled me to a stop on the sidewalk in front of the restaurant and brushed his thumb over my cheek.

"You know, pink is really a lovely color on you."

"Jackson..." I covered his hand on my cheek with my own, looking into his dark eyes. "What is this? What are we doing here?"

I had to know. He was acting like we were a couple, which didn't match what happened this morning one bit. He sighed, and I could tell that he knew what I was asking.

"I don't know, I just kept thinking all day about what happened last night and this morning and...I tried to convince myself that it was best to just forget about sleeping together, but I realized that I didn't want to. Not only that, but I want to take you out on a date. All these women you've set me up with, and the whole time I think that maybe it should've just been you. So, can we act like this *morning* didn't happen instead? Maybe try out this whole date thing?"

I knew that I should say no, it was right on the tip of my tongue. I didn't want to marry him, not if it was going to be fake, and that was the point of sending him on those dates in the first place. But I found myself nodding instead, as if my neck muscles had a mind of their own.

His sexy, genuine smile was enough to seal the deal. We were going to give this a shot.

When we stepped inside, I had a moment of worry that we would have a long wait. There were already six people waiting for seats. But I shouldn't have underestimated Jackson. Not only did he make a reservation, but he slipped the host some cash in a way that was so smooth I almost missed it.

We were at a table in less than ten minutes.

"So, why did you choose this place?" I asked, picking up my menu and scanning it. They had some good food, but it wasn't the type that I thought a life-long rich boy like Jackson would stumble across.

"Actually, this is special to me. I thought you'd like to see the place where I used to eat lunch with my mom every weekend when I was growing up."

I stared at him with wide eyes. It was the first time he'd voluntarily offered any information about his family, and that felt significant. I was barely breathing, afraid to distract him and miss out on this rare glimpse of his past.

"She doesn't live in Charlotte anymore. Moved to California when Chase and I were fully grown, so I don't see her much these days, but she really liked this restaurant. Their rolls and honey butter were her guilty pleasure. After she and my dad divorced, he had primary custody of us, and we saw her on the weekends. I swear, we spent every Saturday night here. I like to still come sometimes because it reminds me of her. She was so much happier after the divorce and bringing us out to eat was a part of that."

"Can I get you guys something to drink, to get started?"

I jolted, not expecting the waitress's voice to break into his story. I hadn't even noticed her arrival. She set down a basket of rolls in the center of the table and pulled out an order pad.

Jackson ordered us a bottle of red wine. The waitress left us alone, and I waited to see if he would tell me more about his past.

"The divorce was ugly," he continued, and I hung on every word. I hadn't even bothered to glance at my menu yet, but I didn't care. My hunger was taking a backseat to my curiosity. "I mean, things were bad in the last year or so of their marriage, but their treatment of each other got really nasty once my mom moved out."

"What's that mean?" I couldn't resist asking.

"The two of them fought bitterly over everything. Their stuff, their money, and most importantly, their kids. Me and Chase were stuck in the middle of all of the animosity they spewed at each other, and by the end of it all, I just couldn't understand how they could say they ever loved each other in the first place."

"How old were you?"

"By the time the divorce was finalized? Ten. They'd dragged it out for two years before that. But that's why I like this place so much. Both of my parents started to heal afterward. I lived with my dad, so it was more obvious with him. For my mom, I saw the anger and hurt melt away every week while we sat here, eating steak and catching up. I know she missed us, but it was so much better for her to be away from my dad. Apart, they aren't bad people, but together... Well, they're toxic."

I thought about what he'd told me about his ex-fiancée. So, his parents split up when he was a kid, damaging his faith in love. Then, he thought he found it for himself, but the woman cheated on him and used him for financial gain and status.

Okay, I was starting to understand his derisive attitude toward romance and love.

The waitress returned with our wine. She put two glasses on the table and uncorked the bottle, pouring a generous amount for each of us. I finally looked at the menu, choosing the first thing listed under the entrees. I wasn't a picky eater, and a ribeye steak sounded pretty good to me. We both placed our orders and she left us again. I sipped my water as I looked at Jackson, waiting to see if he had more to share with me, but he didn't say anything else. His attention was on his drink, staring at it without seeming to actually see it. He looked so vulnerable right now, more so than I'd ever seen him.

"Why are you telling me all this?" I asked. "Don't get me wrong, I'm glad you did, but frankly, I'm shocked."

One side of his mouth quirked up in a half grin. "I guess I'm not exactly an open book, am I?"

I gave him a soft smile. "That would be too boring, anyway."

Silence settled over us again, and Jackson reached across the table to take my hand. Butterflies took flight in my stomach, and I was starting to like his idea of acting like this morning never happened.

"I can't really answer your question," he said. "I didn't really plan to delve into my family history like that. I just wanted to take you somewhere that means something special to me."

I didn't stop to think about it before leaning across the narrow table and pressing a kiss to his lips. It was short, but when I pulled away, there was a flash of heat and desire in his eyes.

"You want to get out of here?" he asked, but at that moment, the waitress returned with our food.

My mouth watered at the sight of juicy steak and asparagus on the plate she sat in front of me. My thoughts must have shown on my face, because Jackson chuckled, shaking his head.

"Okay, fine. Let's eat first."

The food was delicious, the steak cooked perfectly. Jackson's piece of meat was twice as big as mine, but he finished in record time.

"I guess you were hungry," I commented.

"I'm eager to get you out of here."

He was so upfront about what he wanted, and I found that his directness stirred up a different kind of hunger inside of me. Did I really have second thoughts about sleeping with this man just this morning? Maybe it was the wine influencing me, but my reasoning this morning seemed so far away in this restaurant with the low lighting and need pulsating through my body.

"I'm done," I said, refusing to second guess my decision. "Let's go."

I hadn't finished my steak yet, but I didn't care. Jackson stood, pulled out his wallet and tossed down what looked like way too much cash. Our lucky waitress was probably going to end up with a massive tip because we weren't sticking around to wait for change. Jackson took my hand again, and led me out of the restaurant. We'd only been inside for about an hour, but the parking lot had cleared out a lot in that time. Jackson's car was sitting all by itself near the back of the lot, and I let out a light laugh as he pulled me along faster.

"In a hurry?" I teased.

Instead of answering, he stopped and pulled me close. His hand cupped my cheek as he kissed me, making me melt against him. I ached for him to touch me, but we were standing in the middle of the lot. God, I wished we were home already.

Apparently on the same page I was,

Jackson pulled away and led me the rest of the way to the car. The lights flashed as he unlocked it with his key fob, illuminating the darkness surrounding it. The parking lot lights were closer to the building, and I would have been intimidated walking into the shadows alone, but with Jackson by my side, I had no such concerns. I felt safe with him.

Once we were inside the car, I expected him to head home right away, but he didn't. Instead, he twisted in his seat so that he was facing me, and with his hand sliding around the back of my neck, he pulled me to him and kissed me again. This time it was rough, demanding and erotically deep. My palms flattened against his chest, and I closed my eyes, losing myself in the kiss as heat rolled through my body.

Jackson cupped my breast, and I gasped, pulling away from the kiss and looking into his face. Even in the near darkness, I could make out a wicked glint in his eyes.

"Jackson, what are you doing?" I looked out at the parking lot around us, seeing a few people walking to their cars.

"I'm just getting started," he said, moving

his hand into my shirt, the V-neck giving him easy access. He ran his thumb over my hardened nipple through my satin and lace bra. I gasped and shuddered. "Don't worry about those people. No one can see us here. I wouldn't allow it. No one gets to see your pleasure but me."

Tilting his head, he pressed a kiss just below my ear, blowing softly on the skin until every nerve ending in my body flared to life. I knew that I should stop him, that this was risky, and we could easily get caught. But that was part of the thrill of it.

When he moved his hand down my body, unbuttoning my jeans, I couldn't find the words to protest. I wanted it too much.

Jackson kissed along my jawline as he slid his palm over my mound, cupping my pussy. He slipped two long fingers inside of me, and I fisted his shirt, pulling him closer. The only sound in the car was my labored breathing as he started to pump his finger in and out of me.

He knew what he was doing, working me up quickly by thrusting even faster, deeper, with his thumb rubbing across my clit. It felt so good, and doing it here was *wild.* I squirmed in the seat, my hips jutting forward and back, over and over again, as my pleasure soared.

I let out a small moan, trying to stay quiet even though the tinted windows were all rolled up and no one was anywhere near us. A car pulled into the parking lot and the headlights washed over us for a fraction of a second. I'd never considered myself to be much of an exhibitionist, but knowing that someone could see us if they'd been looking our way while we were illuminated pushed me over the edge. The danger of what we were doing made my climax swept through me with little warning.

"Oh, God..." I groaned, my body tensing.

Jackson's mouth was on mine again, his tongue thrusting in and out just as his fingers were. I was surrounded by him as I surrendered to the electric currents of pleasure that ran through me.

It was over too soon, and I wanted more. I wanted to feel him inside of me again.

Jackson pulled his hand away, his eyes locked on mine as he brought his hand to his mouth and slowly licked his fingers clean. I had never seen anything so dirty and erotic in my entire life, and my tongue darted out to lick my own lips.

"You tasted just as sweet as I knew you would," he said, his voice hoarse. "I'm going to take you home now, and you're spending all night long with me, letting me fuck you every way imaginable."

There was no room for argument as he started up the car, leaving me to straighten out my own clothing. That was fine with me. I was done fighting this intense attraction. Bad idea or not, I wanted Jackson Goodman more than I'd ever wanted anything and somehow, I was determined to make him mine.

Chapter Eighteen

Jackson

When I had talked myself into taking Felicity out to dinner tonight, I was hoping to mend fences between us. I didn't plan to fuck her again, knowing that she was completely right about it complicating things, but I didn't factor in the attraction that still burned brightly between us. I had hoped that sleeping together would scratch that itch and diminish the spark.

It didn't.

If anything, I wanted her even more now that I'd gotten a taste of her pussy.

Drake was gone for the night, so when we got home, I didn't waste any time. As soon as the front door was closed behind us, I pressed her up against it right there in the foyer, caging her in with my arms on either side of her body. Not that she tried to get away. I kissed her fiercely while her hands went to the center of my button-down shirt. Gripping it tightly, she tore it open, sending buttons flying everywhere.

Holy shit, that was hot.

Her nimble fingers danced across my skin, down my torso until she reached my belt. Getting with the program, I started to undress her too, and we became a tangle of limbs as we headed into the living room, tearing off clothing and flinging it to the floor while we kissed and touched. We were both naked by the time we reached the couch, and I stopped long enough to turn on a floor lamp in the corner of the room. She was too beautiful to fuck in the dark and I wanted to see every bare inch of her.

"Do you have a condom on you?" she asked breathlessly through kiss-bitten lips.

Damn it.

"Change of plans," I said, scooping her up into my arms and carrying her bridal-style like I did the day she fell in my kitchen. But this time, I took her upstairs, going as fast as I could while she giggled.

"I can walk, you know."

I grinned at her. "But then, how would I impress you?"

This time she laughed, and the sound gave me a feeling of peace in the center of my chest that I'd never experienced before.

When we reached my room, I put her on the bed. I'd never felt so crazed for a woman before, and every second that I wasn't inside of her was torture. I grabbed a condom out of the nightstand, but before I opened it, Felicity grabbed my cock, stroking it slowly as she looked up at me through her eyelashes from her spot sitting on the edge of the bed.

She licked her lips before lowering her head, her tongue darting out to lick up the drop of precum at the tip of my erection. A violent wave of pleasure washed over me, and

I reached out to hold onto her silky brown hair. I growled low in my throat as she took my cock into her mouth, swallowing as much as possible and gripping the base.

"*Fuck,* Felicity..." My head fell back on my shoulders and my breath left me in a low hiss.

Her mouth was hot and wet, and I reveled in the feeling of it wrapped around me. Every once in a while, she pulled back all the way, swirling her tongue around the tip, which sent a jolt of raw ecstasy straight through the center of me.

If she kept going like this, I was going to come into her throat and that wasn't what I wanted. I need to be buried inside of her tonight. Reluctantly, I pulled her off of my cock.

"Get on your hands and knees," I ordered, ripping open the foil packet and rolling on the condom. I had the sudden urge to take her bare, with nothing separating us. I wanted to know what it felt like to be surrounded by nothing but her silky walls.

But I shoved that thought to the back of my mind. I wasn't going to slow things down to have that conversation right now. When we were married, we could talk about birth control options. *Married*, because I knew that this was the only woman I wanted in my life.

Felicity was a gorgeous sight with her ass in the air, her hair tumbling down her arched back, and her legs parted enough to give me a view of her slick pussy. She looked over her shoulder at me with a seductive, come-and-get-me-grin.

"Is this how you want me?" she asked, her voice practically a purr.

"Every. Fucking. Night."

Climbing onto the bed behind her, I lined myself up at her entrance. Grabbing her hips, I drove forward, burying myself all the way inside of her in one smooth thrust. She was so damn tight, and I gritted my teeth as I immediately felt a tightening in my body, the building of an explosive release. No other woman had ever gotten me to this point so quickly before, where I felt as if I could come in just a few thrusts.

There was just something about Felicity that got me going like no one else. I didn't know if it was the sweet curves of her body, the small sounds of pleasure that escaped her full lips each time I rammed my hips forward, or the way that her pussy gripped me like a fist, as if trying to pull the orgasm out of me.

But I wanted this to last, so I took it nice and slow, watching the muscles in her back expand and contract as she rocked forward and back. Her breasts swung freely and I urged her to straighten so that we were both on our knees and I could cup them, her hard nipples pressing into my palms.

I kissed down the side of her neck, and she moaned, reaching back and burying her hands in my hair as I plucked at her nipples with my fingers. A fine sheen of sweat coated my body and the carnal need rushing through my veins gave me a heady feeling. We moved together as one, and I knew that I wouldn't last much longer. It felt too good, and I didn't have the willpower to fight it. But I had to get Felicity there first.

Moving one of my hands down over her stomach, I found her clit, rubbing and circling the taut bud of flesh with my finger. Felicity's small cry of pleasure left no doubt in my mind about what was about to happen. Sure enough, her entire body tensed up and she started to pant.

"Jackson, I'm coming...Oh, my God, I'm going to..." She trailed off as her breath hitched.

I could feel it, the way that her pussy contracted, spasming around my erection until I let out a deep, satisfying groan. My heart was beating fast as my release erupted through me, so hard that I felt lightheaded. I was hurtled in bliss, rutting into her as one hand held her breast and the other kept working her clit, trying to draw out both of our climaxes as long as possible.

When it was over, we both collapsed onto the bed. It took all the energy I had left to get rid of the condom, and turn off the bedside lamp. After that, I pulled Felicity close, settling in under the covers. I was on my back and her head was resting on my shoulder, her arm draped over my abdomen. I pressed a kiss to the top of her head, running my fingers through her hair.

"Jackson?"

"Yeah?"

"Thanks for dinner," she said, her voice sleepy.

I smiled in the darkness. "Thanks for dessert."

She laughed and slapped my chest lightly. The two of us relaxed against each other, and it wasn't long before her breathing became deep and even. I stayed awake for a while, thinking about the woman in my bed. Was she serious about taking the place of my bride?

God, I hoped so. She had signed a contract, and a year of doing this every night to get my trust fund was probably the best damn idea that I'd ever heard. I enjoyed Felicity's company. She was smart and funny and I respected her.

Trust and love weren't necessary, were they? Couldn't I just have a good time with her, make my dad happy, and give her the ability to run her company the way it should be run, with efficiency and a support staff?

Then, everybody would win. I just needed to get her on board with the idea.

* * *

I awoke to the annoying sound of my doorbell ringing. With Felicity wrapped up in my arms, I was having one of the best nights of sleep I could ever remember enjoying. I didn't want to be pulled out of dreamland, and I *really* didn't want to leave the bed.

But if there was someone at the door, what choice did I have? I was the master of the house, so any visitor would be here to see me. I couldn't just ignore it.

Managing to get out of the bed without waking Felicity, I grabbed my pajama pants off the floor and pulled them on before leaving the room and closing the door softly behind me. It was early, and I wanted to give Felicity a chance to sleep a little before she had to get up and get ready for work.

I was halfway down the stairs when Drake pulled open the door to reveal my father, Jackson Goodman II. He went by Jack, and his father, my grandpa, went by Jay when he was alive. But I still wasn't a big fan of sharing my name with them. It felt like an expectation to follow in my father's footsteps was placed on me at birth, and how unfair was that?

Still, he was a shrewd businessman, and I learned a lot from him about how to be successful. I respected the hell out of the man.

"Dad? What are you doing here?" I asked, looking at the grandfather clock in the foyer. It wasn't even eight in the morning yet. I came the rest of the way down the stairs.

"I need to borrow your golf clubs."

"Is there something wrong with yours?" I asked as Drake went to the hall closet where I kept my clubs. He knew me well enough to know that I wouldn't deny my dad any reasonable request.

"No, but I only have the one set, and I'm taking a new lady friend to the club to play a few rounds. She's never played before, so she doesn't have her own."

"A new lady friend?" I asked curiously. "I didn't know you were dating anyone."

"I just met her a couple of days ago, but she's a hell of a looker." Pulling out his phone, he came closer and showed me a picture of a pretty—and young—woman that was making a kissy face to the camera.

"Wow. How old is she?"

"Age is just a number," he said, putting the phone away.

"That young, huh?" I shook my head, folding my arms across my chest. "You know, you've got some nerve telling Chase and I that we need to settle down while you're running around with a woman that's probably younger than both of us."

"Hey, I settled down back in the day—"

"Which was a disaster," I interrupted.

"—and I had my kids. Sons to carry on the family name. That's what's important, you know."

I rolled my eyes as he continued like he didn't hear me interrupt him at all. If there was one thing he didn't like to discuss, it was my mother.

"Yeah well, if you keep dating younger and younger women, maybe you can have another crack at it," I said, not bothering to hide my sarcasm. "Then, you won't need me and Chase to 'carry on the family name.'"

Dad shuddered. "Another kid, at my age? I don't think so."

I laughed at the idea of that. He'd be in

his seventies when the kid graduated from high school.

"Oh." The sound of Felicity's voice drew my eyes to the staircase, where she was halfway down, gripping the railing. She was barefoot with her legs on display since she was only wearing a long T-shirt from my drawer.

That was when I realized that the clothes we shed last night were still all over the floor in the foyer and living room. As if Felicity's appearance dressed that way wasn't obvious enough.

"I'm sorry," she squeaked, looking completely embarrassed as she froze in place. "I was going to get a cup of coffee. I didn't know you had company."

"This is my father," I said, internally amused that we'd already entered the *meet-the-parents* part of all this. "Dad, this is Felicity."

"Uh, hi. It's nice to meet you," Felicity said politely, but I could tell by her expression that she was mortified. "I think I'll just pop back upstairs and put some clothes on.

What a shame.

I watched her go, wondering if she was sore from last night or if I could talk her into a quick round in the shower when my dad left. She'd just crested the top of the stairs and walked out of sight when I felt a nudge in my arm. I turned to see a smile on my dad's face.

"See I knew you just needed a kick in the ass to get the ball rolling," he said smugly. "You keep this up, and you'll have access to your money again in no time."

"What I'm doing with Felicity isn't about that," I said without thinking, shocking myself.

Of course it's about that. I just need a marriage that will give me access to my money.

"Well, that's interesting," Dad replied, studying me like I was one of the crossword puzzles he liked to do on Sunday mornings, a particularly complicated one.

I didn't know what to say to that because I was even more shocked than he was at the words that just came out of my mouth. But Felicity reappeared soon after that, fully clothed in low-cut jeans and a T-shirt. There was a little strip of skin visible on her lower stomach and I bit my lip as my desire flared.

This woman was killing me without even trying. And it wasn't just lust. There was more than that to what we had between us. The money was starting to mean less and less every day.

"Are you joining us for breakfast?" I asked, but Dad shook his head.

"You saw that picture right? She's at the club, and I'm not inclined to keep her waiting."

He left after Drake loaded up my clubs in the trunk, and I checked the time and smiled. We had just enough time to grab a bite to eat and take a shower together before work.

What a perfect way to start the day.

Chapter Nineteen

Felicity

I'd never lived alone, which was probably why I hadn't given much thought to what it would be like to live with a man. There was something about it that made me feel content, a happiness that felt like a warm bubble in the center of my chest. Or maybe that feeling came because the man was Jackson.

Tonight, he arrived home from work just minutes after I did, and the two of us were sitting on the back patio, in the exact same seat that we sat in on the day I arrived. We were strangers then, and I was so uncertain about this whole crazy arrangement. Now, I didn't just know this man, I was developing real feelings for him.

I never expected this to happen when he came storming into my office last week, especially this fast, but that didn't matter. Because I loved him. It was crazy, but I had no doubt it was true. I had always been a big believer in the idea that "when you know, you know."

My mom had told me once that she knew she'd end up marrying my dad by the end of their first date, and they'd been together for forty years. There were no hard and fast rules when it came to this sort of thing, and I knew my own heart well enough to be sure. I had fallen for Jackson. Sleeping together wasn't a mistake, like I said it was. It opened my eyes to the truth of my feelings.

What I had to figure out now was if I should tell him. We were sipping white wine, and I was listening to him talk about his day, but in my mind, I felt like there was a countdown clock, getting closer and closer to a deadline that I'd agreed to in the heat of the moment. If I didn't find a bride for Jackson by Saturday, which was tomorrow, then I was supposed to marry him myself on Sunday.

I was so sure that I wouldn't have to follow through with that, but now I wanted to. I had this wild hope that I could make him love me back within that year we spent together, that I could get my happy ending after all. But it was a big risk. My heart could end up shattered.

I had gone ahead and checked the app today, just like I had been all week, and I came across another candidate that met his criteria. She was just about perfect on paper and based on the way she answered the profile questions, I suspected that she was laid-back enough to go along with this marriage of convenience thing too. But I didn't want to tell Jackson about her.

I hated the idea of walking away from him now. I was going to do it, I was going to take a chance on love because I was pretty sure that Jackson felt the same way about me. He'd never admit it—even to himself—because he was trying to protect himself from being hurt again, but I'd seen the affection in his eyes last night. I knew in my heart that we were meant to be.

"So, you're awfully quiet," he said, and I pulled my speculative gaze away from the twilight glow of the sky. "Tell me about your day."

I smiled, relaxing back into the patio chair. "I signed a contract with a new sponsor today. A publishing company for romance eBooks wants to run their ads on ForeverLuv. They're really excited to be doing business with us, and for the first time ever, we're able to charge a lot of money for the ad space since it's so massively popular."

"You're welcome," he said, taking a mock bow while still sitting in his chair.

I laughed. "No one has ever accused you of being humble, have they?"

"Being humble is overrated. A person should know their worth. You certainly do. I recognized your confidence the moment we met and you pinned me with that impatient, no-nonsense gaze. You know that a rich asshole is not any more important than you are."

"So, you admit that you were an asshole?" I teased.

He smirked. "I'll say that wasn't my finest moment and leave it at that."

Drake came outside to tell us that dinner was ready, so we got up and went into the dining room. He prepared us chicken breasts with a white wine sauce and roasted vegetables, and the two of us started eating while we continued to talk. It felt good to have someone to share my day with, and I filled him in on the party that I was helping my sister plan for my parents' fortieth wedding anniversary next week.

Rose was still angry at me, so we'd been communicating via texts only for the past two days and only talking about the party, but I hoped it would blow over soon. It was hard to be on the outs with her. Jackson was a good listener as I told him all about that. He didn't have any advice to offer, but I felt like a burden had been lifted just by discussing my sister's situation.

After dinner, the two of us went into the living room, sitting on the couch together as we each read a book from his collection—Of Mice and Men for me and a more modern horror novel for him. It was a quiet evening that some people would probably categorize as dreadfully boring, but I enjoyed it. I was comfortable in this house now, and especially with this man. I didn't need a lot of excitement. I just wanted to unwind and relax at the end of my workweek with someone I enjoyed being with.

When I started yawning every couple of minutes, Jackson closed his book and took mine from my hands, announcing that it was time to go to bed. I didn't argue. My eyelids were heavy as we went upstairs, and I paused outside of my room, but Jackson took my hand and pulled me past it. When we got into his room, he stripped down to boxer shorts and handed me a shirt. Turning my back to him, I peeled off my clothes and put it on, loving that the material smelled like him.

When we got into bed together, I expected that he'd initiate sex. Why else would he want me there?

But he didn't. Pulling the blankets over us, he kissed me tenderly. Then, he turned off the light and wrapped his arms around me, pulling me in close. My head was tucked into his broad chest, and I sighed as a feeling of pure contentment washed over me.

"I sleep better with you here," he said softly.

He always seemed to know what I was thinking, and I liked that. It felt like we were in sync, emotionally and physically. "Goodnight, Jackson."

I love you. God, I wanted to say that, but I didn't want to freak him out. I knew that it would take time to build on the affection he felt for me, and I was willing to put in the work to make him realize what we could have together. What we could *be* together.

"Goodnight," he replied, tightening his arms around me for a second, in a way that soothed my soul. When he relaxed his hold, I closed my eyes and listened to the steady beat of his heart as I drifted off to sleep.

I woke up slowly with a lazy smile stretching across my face. I had been having a dream about Jackson—the kind where we were naked on a beach, getting down and dirty in the sand—and it was lingering as I came into consciousness. My body was tingling with pleasure and I was so turned on that I couldn't stand it.

Then, I felt a long, slow lick right up the center of my pussy. I gasped in shock. My eyes flew open and I looked down to see the outline of a head beneath the blanket between my legs.

Jackson.

His hands were on the inside of my thighs, spreading me wide, and I moaned loudly as his tongue slithered inside of me, exploring my most intimate parts before sucking on my clit. It had been so long since a man had given me this kind of erotic pleasure, and never spontaneously like this.

This man was *skilled.*

My eyes shut tight again, and I gripped the sheets on either side of my body, arching my back as he lapped at me. With his broad shoulders keeping my legs wide open, his hands slid up my body and cupped my breasts beneath his shirt. He pinched my tight nipples to add just the smallest undertone of pain that enhanced the pleasure rocketing through me.

I started to circle my hips, riding his talented mouth as I flew closer and closer to the orgasm that I had already been searching for when I opened my eyes. Jackson didn't shy away. If anything, he pressed his mouth harder against me, delved his tongue deeper, consuming me in a way that left me breathless. The stubble of beard he had this morning brushed against my sensitive skin and his nose butt up against my clit.

His name spilled from my lips, and I tightened my legs around his head as I reached the height of euphoria. I was being loud, and I had no idea if Drake was here yet, but I couldn't bring myself to care. Nothing mattered except the slow, thorough way Jackson licked me, taking everything I had to offer as an intense, shuddering orgasm rippled through me.

When he finally pulled away, I felt boneless, laying on my back and breathing erratically while basking in the afterglow of such divine bliss. Jackson whipped back the covers, licking his wet lips as if he'd just eaten something decadent, and looked at me with a sexy, satisfied smile that made my heart somersault.

"Good morning," he murmured, his eyes dancing devilishly.

"Yes, a very good morning, indeed," I agreed huskily.

He smiled affectionately, and again, I had the urge to drop the L word. But again, I suppressed it, knowing he wasn't ready to hear my declaration yet and I didn't want to ruin our morning together.

I thought that he'd grab a condom and take his own pleasure, but instead, he got out of the bed, stretching his arms above his head and making his ab muscles pull tight while his boxers hung low on his hips.

"Where are you going?" I asked, unable to keep the disappointment from my voice, especially since I could see the outline of his erect cock.

He chuckled and leaned down to place a chaste kiss to my lips. "As much as I'd love to stay in bed with you today and do all sorts of dirty things to and with you, I can't. I have a business meeting."

I frowned. "It's Saturday."

"I know, but it's also personal. Chase and his best friend have a business idea that they want me to invest in. They've come up with a whole presentation for me, and I don't want to keep them waiting. Don't worry, I promise we'll pick up where we left off later."

He winked and turned to head to the bathroom. Not sure how to feel, I got out of bed, then went down the hall to my own room, not that I really thought of it that way anymore. I hadn't spent any time in here for days. It was just the room where I kept my things. For now.

If I went through with this wedding tomorrow, this civil ceremony, I assumed that I would officially be sharing a room with Jackson. I bit my bottom lip. I needed to talk to Jackson about this, about *all of it*. I still hadn't even told my family yet.

No sooner had that thought crossed my mind than I got a text from Rose. She wanted to meet in person to go over some anniversary party stuff before we went to spin class together. My heart leapt. I wasn't sure that we were even going to the gym together today, even though we'd been attending the same Saturday afternoon spin class for the past two years. I took her message as a sign that she was ready to stop being mad at me, and quickly texted back a confirmation.

I got in the shower, making sure to shave everything in anticipation of more fun with Jackson later tonight. When I was done, I pulled my damp hair into a messy bun and packed my gym bag.

I figured that Jackson would be gone already, but as I walked out into the hall, I heard his voice coming from his home office with the door ajar. He must have planned the business meeting to take place here since it was his own brother making the presentation. The office was in the opposite direction of the staircase, but I headed in that direction anyway, planning to just pop my head in and tell him that I was leaving but would be back later in the afternoon.

I paused right outside the door when I heard my name and realized Jackson was talking about me. I knew that I shouldn't eavesdrop, but before I could back away, I heard a voice that I recognized as Chase's asking a question that I had to hear the answer to.

"So, you're really going to do it?" his brother asked incredulously. "You're going to marry a woman you barely know?"

"Sure," Jackson said, and I recognized that cold neutrality that his voice could take on sometimes. "That was the plan, right? That I'll do whatever it takes to get my trust fund, even marry my matchmaker."

"Is Felicity okay with that?" Chase sounded skeptical.

"I'm sure she is," he replied confidently. "She signed a contract, and for her, it's all about the money I can put into her company."

"Are you saying she's a gold digger?" Chase asked, and I could hear another layer of doubt in his voice.

Jackson was silent for a long moment, and my stomach dropped. *Was* he saying that?

"I'm just saying that most people only care about how rich I am, and she jumped right on board with this plan when I promised her some money for her company. Draw your own conclusions. It's nothing more than a business arrangement. A win-win situation for both of us."

Now, I backed away, feeling my heart shatter into little pieces in my chest. How could he say that? Did he really think so little of me, especially after the past few days together?

My throat grew tight with tears. God, I was an idiot. I didn't give a shit how rich Jackson was. I honestly believed he cared about me the way that I cared about him, but this whole time, he thought I was just like those people in his life who only wanted him for his money. He had such a low opinion of me, and like an idiot, I'd fallen in love with him.

Biting back the urge to cry, I hurried away, practically running down the stairs and out of the house, away from the man I'd foolishly given my heart to.

Chapter Twenty

Jackson

"I'm just saying that most people only care about how rich I am, and she jumped right on board with this plan when I promised her some money for her company. Draw your own conclusions. It's nothing more than a business arrangement. A win-win situation for both of us."

Chase gaped at me, and I dropped my eyes, not liking the judgement I was seeing in his narrowed gaze. Okay, so I was being a dick. I just couldn't help voicing my fears out loud. I wanted to get Chase's perspective on it because at this point, I was pretty sure that Felicity and I were going to get married. Even if she magically came up with yet another woman from the dating app, I didn't want to meet her.

The only woman I wanted was Felicity.

Suddenly, I thought I heard something out in the hall, the creak of a board. I was standing with my back to the door, but I turned and pulled it open, thinking that Chase's best friend Ben might have arrived. The two of them were planning to go into business as partners, so they wanted to do the presentation together.

No one was in the hallway, so I just left the door open in invitation for him to come in when he arrived and turned back to Chase.

"Do you really mean what you just said?" Chase asked. "Because I only met Felicity once, but I don't know, man. She didn't seem like the gold digging type."

I sighed, crossing to my desk and taking a seat in the high-backed office chair.

"Honestly, I'm not sure what I think," I said, rubbing a hand along the weekend stubble still on my jaw. "I feel like I'm at war with myself. On the one hand, there's my emotions, which you know I don't usually put much stock in, anyway. But they're telling me that she's not only trustworthy, but that she's the perfect girl for me."

"Then, what's the problem?"

"I thought Natasha was perfect too," I said, hating to dredge up that part of my past, but it still haunted me. "Until she cheated and admitted that I was just a way to marry rich. It fucking crushed me. And let's not forget about our parents."

"How could we?" Chase asked bitterly. "The way they decimated each other was one for the history books."

"So, you see why this is hard for me?" I asked, hoping that he understood because I wasn't sure if I was being an asshole myself.

But Chase shook his head. He walked over to a black leather couch that I kept up against the wall and sat down heavily. Leaning forward with his elbow on his knees, he pinned me with a heavy stare.

"I have a confession to make," he started.

This can't be good.

Chase exhaled a deep breath. "I didn't just sign you up for that dating app to mess with you. I wanted to *help* you."

"Help me get a woman? Come on, Chase. We both know how to get women if we want to."

"I'm trying to help you let go of the pain in your past," he said, his tone somber. "Let's get real, here. You don't think love is fake. You *know* it's a real thing. You just hide behind that conviction because love can hurt when it's not with the right person, or it's not reciprocated. But you shouldn't spend your life alone just because you're scared of getting hurt again."

I swallowed a lump in my throat. I didn't want to believe what Chase was saying was true, but it made too much sense to ignore. I'd gotten my ass kicked by love, twice really. My parent's failed attempt at love really messed up my life for a long time, and Natasha's betrayal had been tough to get over. Those fears were real, but somehow, someway, Felicity made me want to *believe* in love again.

"When did you get so smart?" I asked

Chase, and he laughed, breaking some of the heavy tension in the air.

"If you really think that, you should definitely invest in the new business."

There was another creak of the floorboard outside the room, and I looked up to see Chase's best friend, Ben, standing in the doorway. They started their pitch, and I tried to give them my full attention—even though I'd already decided that I would invest in my brother regardless—but my mind was on what Chase said.

Did I really put up a shield of disbelief in the whole institution of love just to protect myself? If so, it wasn't something I did on purpose. I just lost faith in it.

But the bigger question, the one that I kept coming back to, was: did this mean that I was in love with Felicity?

It was six in the evening and Felicity had been gone all day. I didn't know where she was, which was driving me crazy. She wouldn't answer her phone. I knew that she didn't owe me an explanation of where she went or what she did, but I couldn't help being bothered by it.

So I was left waiting impatiently for her to return. While waiting, I noticed for the first time how big and lonely my house was when I was by myself. Just having her here made such a big difference. She somehow brought warmth and light just by being in the house. I couldn't imagine going back to being here alone all the time.

I didn't want her to leave. *Ever.*

The sound of the front door opened, and I hurried out of the living room to see her walking in. I didn't realize just how worried I was that something bad had happened to her until I felt relief flood me. She was a sight for sore eyes.

I came into the foyer to meet her, automatically moving in to give her a kiss, but she took a step back from me. When her blue eyes met mine from behind her glasses, I felt my blood run cold. Something was wrong.

There was a look on her face that I'd never seen before. It was cold and angry, directed at me, and it chilled me to the bone.

"Hey, I was wondering when you'd get home," I said, hoping to somehow wipe that irate look off her face by talking to her. "I tried to call and text..."

"Yeah, I was busy," she said curtly. Then, she sidestepped me and headed to the stairs. I was so surprised by the tone of voice she used that I didn't respond right away.

I had seen her angry before. In fact, that was the first impression I'd ever gotten of her, but that was all defiance and stubbornness and fiery passion. This was different. It was like she was trying to conceal her emotions, to create distance and shut me out.

I didn't like it one bit.

She was already halfway up the stairs, taking them two at a time, and I followed, catching up quickly.

"Felicity, wait. Talk to me," I said, but she didn't even look at me. "What's wrong?"

"Nothing's wrong," she said in a dead voice.

"Bullshit."

We reached the second floor and she went straight for her room, taking quick steps like she was trying to flee from me, but I wasn't going to let her get away that easily. Not until I knew what was wrong so I could fix things.

When she got to her room, the first thing she did was reach under the bed and pull out the suitcase she'd used to bring her stuff over to the house. Unzipping it, she flipped it open and started to pull her clothing out of the dresser drawers. A shocking amount of panic gripped me, and I hurried to her, taking her shoulders and turning her to face me.

"Felicity, what's happening?"

"I'm ready to leave," she said simply, which felt like a punch to the gut. Then, she smiled, but it didn't reach her eyes. "Actually, I have good news. I found you the perfect woman. She'll make a great fake wife."

I recoiled, hurt spreading through me. She picked another woman after all that had happened between us over the last few days?

"I don't want to meet her," I said.

"Well, that's up to you, but either way, I fulfilled my end of the deal. I can't help it if you're being difficult about the women I've found."

"What the hell, Felicity?" I snapped,

getting upset. "Why are you doing this? We were fine this morning, and now you want to see me with someone else? I thought we were past that."

That brought the fire to her eyes, but it wasn't as comforting to see as I thought it would be. She looked livid.

"You should be happy that you're not stuck with some gold-digging matchmaker that's supposedly after your goddamn money."

Oh, shit.

At that moment, I knew that she'd overheard part of my conversation with Chase this morning. That she'd been the one I'd heard by the door. I wanted to kick my own ass, but self-hatred could come later. Right now, my mind was scrambling, trying to think of a way to get her to stay.

I wouldn't physically stop her, so that meant that I had to talk her into it, despite how furious she was. Watching her resume packing and feeling helpless, I knew that Chase was right. I was scared to love, and now I knew that not only was love real, but I was about to lose the real deal if I didn't get my shit together.

"I'm sorry. But I swear, I didn't mean what I said," I attempted, my voice hoarse. She didn't even look my way as she finished stuffing her things into the suitcase, zipping it up and taking it off the bed. "I was just being an insecure asshole. Please, don't go."

But I could see that my words were pointless. She'd already made up her mind about me, and I completely deserved it. She headed for the door, and I stayed there next to her bed, my muscles like iron bands holding me in place. She finally paused in the doorway and turned back to me.

"By the way," she sneered, "you can keep your damn investment money. I'd rather lose *everything* than take a single dime from you."

Then, she was gone.

Chapter Twenty-One

Felicity

There was nothing quite as painful as celebrating the love of a happily married couple while your own heart was a broken mess. The party for my parents' anniversary was at their house, where I was living again.

I missed Jackson's place. Not just because everything was expensive and fancy. I missed Drake, who took his job so seriously and seemed to actually love it. I missed that peaceful back patio. But most of all, I missed Jackson. Our low-key evenings hanging out, waking up in his arms, even arguing with him when he was being pig-headed.

It had been three days since I left Jackson's house, and I hadn't responded to a single text or call he'd made. It was funny, I couldn't stop thinking that if things had gone the way they were supposed to, I would be married to him right now.

Despite everything, a part of me wished that I'd stuck around and gone through with it. It was the small, hopeful part that had been trampled, but still kept a flicker of belief in Jackson and love. That part of me wondered if Jackson would have grown to love me when he realized that I wasn't interested in his money. Maybe I could have convinced him that love was real, after all.

But for the most part, I knew that was foolish, wishful thinking. I had done the right thing by leaving. I would have just ended up hurt even worse if I let myself fall deeper in love with a man that didn't feel the same and never would.

I also couldn't help wondering if he was

going to go out with the last woman I found for him. Would they get married?

I really tried hard not to think about that, especially today. I was at a party, after all. The last thing I wanted was to be a downer on my parents' big day. It was bad enough that I wasn't sure if The Femme Code would survive without the money I was expecting from Jackson. I knew that Madison and Christine were devastated when I told them that the deal fell through without giving any details, and it made me feel like the bad guy for making that decision, but I just couldn't do it. My pride wouldn't let me take the money when Jackson already thought so little of me.

It was a lot of stress and sadness to deal with, but I tried to be present at the party and engage with people. The gathering was being held in our backyard, which was surrounded by an eight-foot privacy fence. There was a banner hanging from the posts that said *Happy Anniversary* and a couple of long tables, one full of food that we'd had catered and other was for presents. There was karaoke on the deck and games in the yard.

The adults played bocce ball and lawn darts while kids threw water balloons at each other and played with nerf guns.

Basically, it was chaotic and crowded, but so much fun. My parents had huge smiles on their faces, which was the most important thing.

I had finally gotten a plate of food, but all the seats were taken outside, so I headed into the house, where far fewer people were congregating, mostly just adults having conversations away from all the party noise. I sat at the dining room table, nibbling on chicken wings and fresh fruit, when the doorbell rang. I was surprised to hear it since I thought all the party guests had already arrived and most of them wouldn't use the doorbell, anyhow. They'd just walk right in.

Leaving my food behind, I went to the door and opened it. I felt like the wind had been knocked out of me when I saw Jackson standing there. I wasn't expecting this, especially not today. There were thirty party guests in this house right now, and I didn't need to be upset in front of all of them.

"What are you doing here?" I hissed.

Jackson was looking over my shoulder into the house. Then, he glanced at the street, which was lined on both sides with cars.

"Oh, no," he said apologetically. "Today's your parents' party, isn't it?'

"Can you just go?" I asked tiredly, remembering the night that I told him about the party and how happy I'd been just to be spending time with him.

"I'm sorry, I can't. I've stayed away long enough to give you time to cool down, but now I have to talk to you."

"Now?" I didn't bother keeping the exasperation from my voice. "Really?"

"Yes."

I narrowed my eyes at him. I wanted to say no, but I was curious about what he might have to say. He was right about me needing to cool off. I hadn't been willing to listen to a single word that came out of his mouth the night I left. Now, I wanted to know what he had to say for himself.

"Fine," I said stiffly, moving out of the way so that he could walk into the house. "Follow me."

I led him to my bedroom, which was the

only place that we could hope for any semblance of privacy right now. I let him inside, then closed and locked the door. Brushing my hair off my face, I took a moment to collect myself while my back was to him. Then, I turned around and found him on one knee in front of me.

My heart beat wildly and my mouth dropped open as I watched Jackson pull a little black box from his pocket and hold it up to me. He opened it, revealing a princess cut diamond that sparkled in the light. Confusion coursed through me.

"Felicity Wright, will you marry me?" he asked earnestly.

Was he out of his mind?

To my horror, tears burned my eyes. "No."

Jackson's eye went wide, and I saw that same hurt that had been there the morning after we had sex for the first time and I had suggested that it was a mistake. But how could he have expected a different answer after the way things ended between us?

"No?" he repeated, standing up with the open box still in his hand.

"I can't marry you, Jackson. I *won't.*" I swiped impatiently at the tears that were leaking from my eyes. Man, this hurt. "That's why I found you another match. I just can't marry someone that's not in love with me, and certainly not for some stupid business arrangement."

"But you're wrong about that," he said, reaching out and gently wiping away my tears with his thumb. "Despite all of my resistance to it, all of my firm beliefs about love, I *did* fall for you. It took you walking away and facing the realization that I might lose you forever to make me realize the truth. I love you, Felicity Wright."

I couldn't let myself believe what he was saying. I'd already tried to convince myself that he felt that way once, and it was devastating to realize he didn't. I couldn't let myself get hurt again.

"No," I shook my head and folded my arms over my middle to hold myself together. "You're just saying that because you need a wife to get your trust fund back."

Jackson's jaw tightened and he took a step closer, invading my personal space with his heat, his stare, the smell of his spicy cologne. But I didn't step back. Instead, I looked up into his intense stare.

"You're wrong," he said with so much earnest conviction that I had to believe it was the truth. "I don't give a damn about the money anymore. All I want, all I need, is *you*. You can have it all, if you'll marry me."

My doubt lingered, but as I held his eyes, all I could see was sincerity. Not once had Jackson ever lied to me, and I so wanted to believe that was true now, too.

"Do you really mean that?" I asked timidly, that flicker of hope turning into a damn inferno inside of me.

"Yes. A thousand times, yes," he stated, a vulnerable emotion in his gaze. "All the money in the world means nothing without you by my side."

The tears came faster now, my feelings overflowing as I threw my arms around his neck, holding on tight as I kissed him with everything I had, trying to communicate without words just how much I loved him.

I couldn't believe this was really happening. It felt like a dream.

When I pulled back, wiping away the stupid tears again, Jackson was wearing his genuine smile, the one I loved so much.

"So, is that a yes?" he asked, already knowing the answer.

I laughed. "I love you, Jackson Goodman. Of course, it's a yes." I pointed my finger at him, jabbing him lightly in the chest. "*But* I don't want to get married at the courthouse. I want a real wedding."

Jackson grabbed my hand that was pointing at him and slipped the ring on my third finger. It was a perfect fit.

"Of course," he said, grinning happily. "That's how love works, right? You get anything you want."

I squeezed his hand. "All I want is you."

Epilogue

Jackson

"I now present to you, Mr. and Mrs. Goodman."

As the minister said those words, everyone stood up from their white chairs and cheered. I held Felicity's left hand, now bearing a thin wedding band along with the engagement ring I gave her a month ago, while her other hand held a bouquet of pink roses.

The two of us led the way back down the aisle, our bridesmaids and groomsmen trailing along behind. There were two hundred people packed into the botanical garden for the wedding, but I only had eyes for one woman. My bride. My love. My life and my future.

Felicity was stunning in a sleeveless white dress with a tight, beaded top and a skirt that flared out at the waist, brushing the ground as she walked. It was the perfect dress to show off her curvy body, and I couldn't wait to get her alone. But first, there was some partying to do.

There was a banquet hall on the property where we were holding the reception, and when I walked inside, I couldn't believe how perfect it was. I wasn't exactly into wedding decor, but even I was impressed. Allison had teamed up with Rose and the two of them had put the reception together for us, so it was the first time we were seeing it. Round tables with white tablecloths, twinkle lights draped from the ceiling, long-stemmed white candles as centerpieces...it was exactly what Felicity wanted.

As for me, I was happy as long as she was happy.

I had no problem giving her the beautiful wedding she wanted, but I had one condition. I wanted it done quickly. It wasn't because of the trust fund, either. Now that I'd opened myself up to love again, I was determined to never let it go. I wanted Felicity to be mine in every way possible. My lover, my friend, my wife. It had been a wild ride, but the whole thing came together in a month, and now here we were, husband and wife. She was all mine and I was all hers.

"Congratulations," Chase said, coming up and cuffing me on the shoulder. "You're one lucky man."

Chase was my best man, and I knew that I owed a lot to him. I never would have met Felicity if it wasn't for his meddling in my personal life. I'd been so annoyed with him when it happened, and now, I was just thankful. Signing me up for that app had completely changed my life for the better.

"Yeah," I agreed, still staring at Felicity while she hugged her parents. We were standing near the entrance to the banquet hall, and all the wedding guests were lined up to congratulate us. "I am."

I couldn't believe that I'd almost missed out on this because I was too damn stubborn to see that Felicity was the perfect woman for me all along. Not the perfect fake bride, the perfect woman to spend my life with. I'd managed to find Miss Wright, and I wasn't even looking for her.

"Well, son, I'm proud of you," my dad said, grasping my hand and giving me a half hug. "I'll admit, I was a little worried that you'd pay someone to marry you or something like that just to get the trust fund, but I can tell by the way you two look at each other that you've found love."

"Yeah, I..." My voice trailed off as I saw who was approaching from behind him. *Oh no.*

"Jackson, sweetheart, I'm so happy for you," my mom said, coming to a stop right next to my dad. I felt like I was in the twilight zone as I stared between the two of them, and I sensed that Chase was having the same shocked reaction next to me.

My parents were hardly ever in the same space together since their divorce was finalized, but when they were, it always led to an embarrassing and volatile fight between the two of them. The last time I could remember it happening was when I was sixteen and broke my leg playing football. They both came to the hospital, and it had been mortifying to watch them pick at each other until they were in a screaming match and had to be escorted out by security.

So, for my wedding day, I had threatened to cut them both off from any future grandchildren if they got into a fight and ruined our day. I expected them to avoid each other like the plague, but here they were, side-by-side. I watched as they politely greeted each other, actually getting along. Or at least, pretending to. Either way, it felt like a freaking miracle.

My parents moved on, and Chase and I exchanged a baffled look before more people came over to congratulate Felicity and I. I felt like I'd hugged about a million people by the time we came to the end of the reception line.

The last two were Madison and Christine. I'd gotten to know the pair of them well over the last month. After Felicity and I got engaged, I'd insisted on going through with the capital investment in The Femme Code and it was a good thing I did because the company was growing at a fast rate and they needed the money to finally upgrade their servers.

The dating app was an even bigger success now than it was a month ago. Who would have thought that people would love the story of the billionaire meeting the love of life in his matchmaker so much? It brought even more publicity to the app, and Felicity adored the idea of our love story helping so many others find their happily ever after.

The food was served, and it was delicious, but I only picked at it, too nervous to eat. I wasn't usually like this, confidence was what I was known for, but I was about to step way out of my element in front of a lot of people.

After everyone had eaten, the DJ started to play a lively love song. Felicity had graciously agreed not to do a first dance with me, knowing that I wasn't a dancer and would be uncomfortable with it.

What she didn't know was that I took lessons for three weeks. I stood and held out my hand. Felicity looked at me with wide, surprised eyes.

"Are you going to leave me hanging in front of all these people?" I asked lightly. She took my hand and I pulled her up out of her chair, leading her to the dance floor.

"What the hell?" She was shocked as I spun her around the dance floor, going through the routine that I'd practiced and practiced until it was perfect.

"Surprise, baby," I grinned, and her smile lit up the room.

"I can't believe you learned to dance for our wedding!"

"For you, wife. I learned to dance for *you*."

"I'm starting to think you've been a secret romantic all along."

I laughed as I dipped her. "You're the only one that can bring out this side of me."

"I love you," she said.

Now, that was something I'd never get tired of hearing. Our song came to an end and everyone applauded before joining us on the dance floor. The music slowed down and we swayed together, my hands on her hips and hers around my neck.

"Hey, who's that woman Chase is with?"

Felicity asked, jerking her head in the direction of the exit. "She's very pretty."

I looked in that direction just in time to see that Chase was fixing to get himself into some trouble. I shook my head as the two of them slipped out the door, mostly unnoticed.

"That's Kat McCarthy," I said. "Chase must be out of his mind if he's sneaking around with her."

"Why?"

"Because hooking up with your best friend's sister is never a good idea," I said, shaking my head.

"The heart wants, what the heart wants," my wife said, clearly full of romance on her wedding day.

I laughed. "Umm, yeah, I don't think this has anything to do with his heart, but rather what's in his pants. They don't call my brother, 'Chase—let the good times roll—Goodman', for no reason."

The song ended at that moment, and the DJ announced that it was time for the bouquet and garter tosses. The dance floor cleared while we stayed in the middle. On one end of the space a group of single women lined up to try to catch the bouquet, while single men did the same thing on the other side. They'd try to catch the garter when I took it off Felicity's leg. Supposedly, the ones to catch the items would be the next to get married.

As I waited for Felicity to toss the bouquet so that I could reach up her skirt for that garter, I thought that it didn't really matter that Chase was missing it. He'd already made it clear that he wouldn't be getting married anytime soon. My little brother might have signed me up for true love, but he had no interest in finding it himself.

Except, I knew that stubborn mindset could easily change. As I'd learned, love happened when you least expected it.

And I had a feeling it would be no different for Chase.

Don't miss Chase Goodman's story in THE BILLIONAIRE'S WEDDING HOOK-UP!

Subscribe to my newsletter to receive a **FREE BOOK** not available anywhere else!

* * *

ALL BOOKS IN THE BILLIONAIRE BROTHER SERIES

The Billionaire's Back-up Wife

The Billionaire's Wedding Hook-Up

ALL BOOKS IN THE IRRESISTIBLE LOVE SERIES

Irresistible Nights

Irresistible Affair

Irresistible Seduction

Irresistible Flirtation

Irresistible Attraction

Irresistible Promises

FOLLOW KAYLEE MONROE ON THE INTERNET:

Kaylee Monroe Newsletter Sign-up

Kaylee Monroe BookBub

Kaylee Monroe Amazon Author Page

Kaylee Monroe Facebook Author Page

Kaylee Monroe Instagram

Kaylee Monroe Goodreads

Made in the USA
Las Vegas, NV
03 February 2022

42938681R00148